Mom swerved back into ou▮ "Leaving Newbury gives us a chance to ▮▮▮▮ selves."

"I don't need to define myself."

"If you don't do it, somebody else will do it for you," said Mom.

"I know who I am," I said.

I thought of a quote that Frank had posted on his office door. He and my father had covered the entrance to the Triple J janitor's office with Post-its and index cards that held poems, sayings, and, as Frank described them, assorted words of wisdom. "'When you drive away from everything you know,'" I recited from memory, "'you leave behind the mirrors that tell you who you are.'"

"Who said that?" Mom asked.

"I just did."

"I mean who said it first."

I shrugged. "I read it on Frank's office door."

"Dulcie," said Mom, "life is bigger than the janitor's door."

"Mom," I answered. "It's a pretty big door."

OTHER BOOKS YOU MAY ENJOY

Best Foot Forward	Joan Bauer
Every Man for Himself	Nancy Mercado, ed.
Guitar Girl	Sarra Manning
Hope Was Here	Joan Bauer
Storky: How I Lost My Nickname and Won the Girl	D. L. Garfinkle
Thou Shalt Not Dump the Skater Dude and Other Commandments I Have Broken	Rosemary Graham
Thwonk	Joan Bauer
The Truth About Forever	Sarah Dessen

defining

dulcie

paul acampora

speak

An Imprint of Penguin Group (USA) Inc.

SPEAK

Published by the Penguin Group

Penguin Group (USA) Inc., 345 Hudson Street, New York, New York 10014, U.S.A.

Penguin Group (Canada), 90 Eglinton Avenue East, Suite 700,
Toronto, Ontario, Canada M4P 2Y3 (a division of Pearson Penguin Canada Inc.)

Penguin Books Ltd, 80 Strand, London WC2R 0RL, England

Penguin Ireland, 25 St Stephen's Green, Dublin 2, Ireland
(a division of Penguin Books Ltd)

Penguin Group (Australia), 250 Camberwell Road, Camberwell, Victoria 3124,
Australia (a division of Pearson Australia Group Pty Ltd)

Penguin Books India Pvt Ltd, 11 Community Centre, Panchsheel Park,
New Delhi - 110 017, India

Penguin Group (NZ), 67 Apollo Drive, Rosedale, North Shore 0632, New Zealand
(a division of Pearson New Zealand Ltd)

Penguin Books (South Africa) (Pty) Ltd, 24 Sturdee Avenue,
Rosebank, Johannesburg 2196, South Africa

Registered Offices: Penguin Books Ltd, 80 Strand, London WC2R 0RL, England

First published in the United States of America by Dial Books,
a member of Penguin Group (USA) Inc., 2006
Published by Speak, an imprint of Penguin Group (USA) Inc., 2008

1 3 5 7 9 10 8 6 4 2

THE LIBRARY OF CONGRESS HAS CATALOGED THE DIAL BOOKS EDITION AS FOLLOWS:
Acampora, Paul.
Defining Dulcie / Paul Acampora.
p. cm.
Summary: When sixteen-year-old Dulcie's father dies, her mother makes a decision
to move them to California, where Dulcie makes an equally radical decision
to steal her dad's old truck and head back home.
ISBN: 0-8037-3046-2 (hardcover)
[1. Grief—Fiction. 2. Death—Fiction. 3. Family life—Fiction.
4. Moving, Household—Fiction. 5. Runaways—Fiction.] I. Title.
PZ7 + [Fic]—dc22 2005016186

Speak ISBN 978-0-14-241183-4

Printed in the U.S.A.

Designed by Teresa Kietlinski • Text set in Fairfield

For Debbie,
Nicholas,
&
Gabrielle

CHAPTER 1

IF THIS WERE A MOVIE, I'd probably have to kill off my father in the very first scene.

Dad's a good-looking guy. I'm thinking young Harrison Ford dressed in a light-blue custodian cover-all. On the big screen, Dad would pour two powerful yet chemically incompatible cleaning solutions into a pink plastic bucket. He'd dip a rough sponge into the pail, then kneel to scrub a stubborn stain off the checkerboard tile on a boys' bathroom floor. With his attention on the tiles, Dad wouldn't notice the deadly yellow-green chlorine cloud rising up from the new poisonous soup behind him. We'd hear the *shhhh-shhhh-shhhh* of his scouring pad on the floor. The camera would pull back into a long shot. Then Dad would keel over, choke, and die.

Death by inadvertent, self-inflicted mustard gas attack.

It would be a fantastic scene. Scary and weird and exciting. It would be even better if it were not all true.

Really.

It happened less than a year ago inside my school, John Jacob Jerome High School, in Newbury, Connecticut, and here's the thing: It never ever felt like a movie.

Not even for a minute.

And yet Dad's accidental demise fast-forwarded me into some kind of real-life-meets-Cartoon-Channel thrill ride, a crazy collection of episodes and moments that made me pause in front of small mirrors and whisper, "Dulcie, are you all right?"

The girl in the reflection usually answered, "I think so." But sometimes she'd stare back and say, "Define 'all right.'"

Look at that girl in the mirror and you'd see your basic sixteen-year-old, average height, and a runner's build, which is a nice way of saying skinny without meaning sickly-looking. For me, "all right" used to include pushing a giant electric floor buffer or dragging massive, drippy garbage bags out of cafeteria trash cans. I was a John Jacob Jerome High School janitor like my dad. So far I'd lived to tell about it.

The Triple J also employed my grandfather Frank Morrigan. Frank was my mother's father, my father's boss, and my boss too. Frank was also king of all things custodial. "A dozen U.S. janitors accidentally poison themselves every year," Frank told us at Dad's funeral. "According to the federal government, six percent of all school cleaning products are so toxic, you can use them as deadly weapons."

"Is that supposed to make us feel better?" my mother asked.

"Yes," said Frank. "Actually, it is."

In a way, those facts did make me feel better. I'd watched my father patch, polish, and repair almost anything that John Jacob Jerome threw his way. I knew that he was not dumb. He'd just made a mistake. Everybody makes mistakes. Of course, some mistakes are more serious than others.

My own custodial duties were much simpler than Dad's. My hours were a lot shorter too. I usually just worked vacation days and after school. But that didn't mean I didn't take the job seriously.

"Dulcie," Dad called to me once when he saw me struggling with a cafeteria trash can. "Do you need a hand?"

I tried not to wrinkle my nose at the smell of

soggy bread and sour milk. Then, like a cowgirl roping a calf, I swung the overfilled garbage bag out of the barrel, wrestled the trash to the floor, and tied it up in knots. "I can handle it."

"Is there anything you can't handle?" Dad asked.

I shrugged.

"You're just like your mom."

"Do you mean I'm a lunatic?"

"I meant that you're strong. A lunatic is a person who becomes wildly giddy or foolish during a particular phase of the lunar cycle." Dad always had a worn dictionary within arm's reach, and he wasn't afraid to use it. "Have you ever known your mother to become wildly giddy or foolish?"

"No," I admitted.

Mom was an expert hairdresser who spent most of her days on her feet, arms suspended above her waist, body held high over her customers. Her shoulders, biceps, and backside were solid muscle, and as far as I could tell, she believed with total certainty that every thought, word, or opinion that made its way out of her mouth was absolutely true.

Still, it took me by surprise when Mom announced that following Dad's funeral, she and I would be moving to California. We were at the funeral home shopping for a casket and a grave marker when Mom let me know about her big decision. I sat down on a big piece of granite carved into the shape of a life-sized Great Dane. All I could think to say was: "What about Dad?"

"He has to stay," said Mom. "We don't."

"We're just going to leave him in Newbury?"

"Whether we leave him here or not won't change things for your father." Mom pointed at the stone dog. "I don't think you should be sitting on that."

I patted the statue's head. "Dad always wanted a dog."

"You think we should get it?"

I imagined Marmaduke standing over Dad's chest for the rest of eternity. "He didn't want one that bad."

We were both quiet for a moment.

"Dulcie," Mom finally said, "a change will be good for both of us."

I took a big breath and let it out slowly. "Isn't losing Dad enough of a change?"

"It's more than enough, Dulcie. It's too much."

For a moment Mom looked like she might cry, but then she pulled herself together. I followed her back to Dad's truck, a 1968 Chevy pickup with a steering wheel as big around as an extra-large pizza and a bench seat the size of a living room couch.

Before he died, Dad had painted the truck fire engine red and dropped a Corvette engine under the hood to make it go. On weekends, he and I worked on the truck inside the John Jacob Jerome auto shop, one of us holding a work light, the other turning a wrench. Dad liked to say that we could drive that truck to the moon and back.

"I don't want to go to the moon," I told him. "I'm happy right here."

"Here inside the Triple J?"

"Here in Newbury," I said. "Here with you."

Dad pulled his head out from beneath the truck's hood and smiled. "Dulcie Morrigan Jones," he said "I think that you are destined for travels and adventure."

If he only knew.

Maybe he did.

Dad used to tell me that Dulcie was Latin for sweet. Morrigan, besides serving as my mother's maiden name, is the Celtic goddess of love and war. As far as Jones, it's slang for avid desire or burning hunger. It's also the most common, ordinary, and uninteresting name in America. "That's why we stuck Dulcie and Morrigan onto the front of it," Dad explained to me while we worked on the truck. "We didn't want you to grow up dull." He paused. "Your mother doesn't like dull."

That would explain why she married my father.

Dad was never dull. He liked practical jokes. He was a painter and a photographer who loved to show off his work. He put himself through college by pushing a mop, but then, according to Mom, he forgot that he was supposed to put his cleaning bucket away. "Why quit now?" Dad asked. "I'm just getting good at it."

"You should be teaching kids, not picking up their trash," said Mom.

"Everybody in a school is an abecedarian," Dad told her.

"A what?" asked Mom.

Dad waved his pocket Webster's at her. "An advisor, an instructor, a swami, an educator."

"Okay, swami," said Mom, "but you could do better."

"I like my job," said Dad.

"You like the free art supplies and the school photo lab," said Mom.

He shrugged. "That too."

I would give anything to see my dad again. I guess

you could say it's my jones, my avid desire, my burning hunger. But I know that's not going to happen. Even if this were a movie, it wouldn't be *Janitor Returns from the Dead*.

On the day that Mom and I left Newbury, we stopped at my grandfather's to say good-bye. We found Frank sweeping the sidewalk that ran alongside his house.

"This is what you do in your free time?" Mom asked her father.

Frank turned to face her. "This isn't right," he said. "Dulcie doesn't have to go. She could stay here with me."

"No," said Mom.

"California," said Frank. "Home to Arnold Schwarzenegger and great white sharks and Mr. Walter Disney's head. Is it really going to be home to you? Is it really where you want to raise my grand-daughter?"

"Dad," said Mom. "We'll be fine."

Frank leaned his broom against a tree. He took a step around Mom and then put his arm around me. For a moment, I thought he was going to toss me over his shoulder like a bag of woodchips and just take me back to the Triple J. Instead, he whispered in my ear, "Don't worry, Dulcie. You always have a home here."

As we rolled out of town, Mom gripped the steering wheel like she was trying to strangle a chicken. I stared into the passenger-side mirror at my grandfather growing smaller in the distance. Then I watched the suitcases and cardboard boxes piled high in the bed of the truck. A flap on one carton started to blow loose, and just as we made a sharp left-hand turn onto the interstate, the box burst open. Stockings and socks and underwear, both mine and Mom's, sailed into the breeze. "Dulcie," Mom said, unaware of the undergarment parade behind us, "it's going to be okay. We're going to be all right."

"Maybe," I said, "but we're not going to be comfortable."

CHAPTER 2

AMERICA IS BIG. REALLY big. It reaches farther, wider, and taller than they ever tell you in school or that you'd ever guess from just looking at it on a map. And if I didn't notice the huge stretch of miles between Connecticut and California on the long drive westward, I sure noticed it a few weeks later when I stole Dad's truck and drove back to Newbury all by myself.

I hadn't exactly planned on abandoning Mom in California. We got settled pretty quickly, found a nice apartment; Mom didn't have any problem finding work. She was tired by the end of her first day at the new job, however, and I was cranky too.

"How was your day?" Mom asked when she got home.

It was late June, and I'd tried to relax at the apartment complex pool. Instead, I spent most of the day worrying about toddlers whose mothers weren't watching them closely enough near the deep end.

"Fine."

Mom pulled a rubber band out of her long pony-tail. Her hair was a rich chocolate brown. It had been light orange just a couple days earlier. My mother changed hair color the way some people change shoes. "Aren't you going to ask about mine?"

"And how was your day?" I asked.

Mom disappeared into our little kitchen. "Cut, curl, rinse, dye," she called to me. "California ladies definitely tip better than my Connecticut customers ever did." We had been away from Newbury for less than a month, and Mom already believed that every-thing was better in California.

I closed the book I was reading and walked out to the little patio stuck onto the back side of our San Leandro apartment. Mom followed. "Don't you love this view?" she asked.

Our apartment was surrounded by the wide, honey brown hills of northern California. From the patio, we could see a huge expanse of sky above, city below, and the San Francisco Bay in the distance. Late-afternoon sun reflected off the faraway water, and tiny dots, sailboats I guessed, were visible on the mirror surface. Along the far western horizon, a soft bank of foggy gray clouds waited to roll over us. In the morning, the chill of that same fog drifting back toward the Pacific Ocean would leave the air fresh and cool. It was all so different from the rock-strewn fields and summer green maples that I was used to. This place begged to be loved.

"It's okay," I said.

"Dulcie," Mom said. "I want to tell you something."

I kept my eyes on the horizon. "What is it?"

"I stopped at a Volvo place on the way home from work. I was just going to look, but guess what?"

I didn't answer, so she continued.

"I ordered one of those little station wagons. I'm getting rid of the truck."

"Dad's truck?"

"Actually," she said, "it's my truck now."

"We crossed the country in that truck."

"Yes," said Mom. "We did."

I took a big breath. There was no way I was going to let Mom throw away Dad's Chevy.

"A small car just makes more sense," Mom said.

"Mom," I said carefully. "We don't have a lot of things left that belonged to Dad."

"We have each other, Dulcie."

I closed my eyes and tried to calm myself. "I don't mind driving the truck. You could give it to me."

"You can't drive that thing around here. There's too much traffic."

"I thought everything was better in California."

"Be reasonable," said Mom.

"I am reasonable," I said, "and I'm a good driver." That was true. Dad and Frank taught me to drive in the Triple J parking lot before I turned fifteen. "You let me drive the truck when we moved out here," I added.

Mom sighed. "That was different. I was falling asleep at the wheel."

"So I'm trustworthy when you're putting our lives in danger, but the everyday commute is too much."

"Dulcie," said Mom. "The morning drive through Nebraska is a little different than rush hour around here. And by the way, you're the kid. I'm the mom. I don't need your permission to buy a new car."

"You just don't want anything left that reminds you of Connecticut."

"I just don't want to drive a farm vehicle anymore."

I was close to tears, so I didn't speak.

"Listen," Mom said. "The man at the car dealer

told me he never offered anybody less than a thousand bucks for a trade-in that ran. Guess what he offered me for the truck."

"What?"

"Three hundred dollars."

She laughed. She actually laughed. I clamped my teeth together so that I would not say something terrible.

"With a new car, we won't have to scare pedestrians when our bumpers fly off. We'll be able to find a parking spot in the city for a change. I won't have to fork over half my pay just to fill the gas tank."

"We're throwing away the last thing that belonged to Dad," I said.

"That's not true."

"It is."

I stared off the patio and studied the view. Somehow, the beauty of it made me even more angry. I did not hate California. I really didn't know much about it yet, but the thought of the ocean on the left side of the map rather than the right was dizzy and annoying. California weather that promised to stay the same for weeks and weeks was almost as unsettling as the tall ridges and invisible fault lines that I understood could quake and crack open beneath me at any moment. This was not New England. This was not me. This was not my home.

"Dad loved that truck," I said.

"He's not using it anymore," said Mom.

A quick flash of anger made my face burn. And then suddenly I knew what I would do. It was like I heard the snap of a switch clicking into place or the flap of a kite sail suddenly catching a breeze. "Okay," I said. "Fine."

"Then it's settled," said Mom. "I pick up the Volvo the day after tomorrow."

I shrugged. "Okay," I said again. "I guess you're going to need it."

That night, I barely slept. I thought of the socks and clothes blown in our wake as we left Newbury. Mom hadn't even noticed what had happened until the empty carton bounced out of the truck. She laughed then and told me, "There's nothing back there that we can't buy new." For Mom, Dad's big Chevy was just the same as those clothes, just one more thing to lose or throw away and replace.

I climbed out of my bed and went to the window. Below me, it looked like all of California was asleep. Fog had rolled in and the chill of it seeped through my windowpane. I was still thinking about that missing underwear. It reminded me of the crumbs and pebbles Hansel and Gretel dropped to help them find their way home. Of course, things had not gone quite the way they planned. Abandoned by their own parents. Nearly cooked and eaten by a witch. But everything had worked out for them in the end, hadn't it?

Before I could change my mind, I slipped on a pair of jeans and pulled a sweatshirt over my head. I grabbed a blanket, a few of Dad's old books, some clean clothes, and I stuffed the whole bundle into a bag. I found keys on the kitchen counter and slipped a credit card out of Mom's purse. On a scrap of paper, I jotted down a quick note:

I owe you three hundred dollars.

And then I left.

It was easy. I knew it would be. Mom had showed me how. Despite all the connections, all our memories, all the history, she'd pulled us out of Newbury like a tow truck pulling Dad's Chevy out of a ditch. Thanks to Mom's less than amazing driving skills, I'd seen that event more than once. It seemed like an impossible task, but it was not.

There was even a part of me that believed I was doing my mother a favor. Except for the truck, I figured

I was the last thing left that she'd brought to California from Connecticut. With her new car, her new apartment with a view, a new job, and me gone, she'd have a slate as clean as any newly washed blackboard.

I tiptoed down the apartment steps and slipped behind the wheel of the big red pickup. The key turned easily in the ignition and the big V-8 hummed to life.

Glancing toward Mom's dark window, I half hoped the truck would backfire. Dad never had tuned the engine quite right, and sometimes a blast would come out of the tailpipe loud enough to make cows give bad milk for a week. I imagined a lamp blinking to life in the apartment, then Mom bursting out the door and running toward the curb. If that had happened, I don't know whether I would have jumped down from the cab or shoved the gas pedal to the floor. I let the pickup idle for a moment while I considered it.

The sky was turning from black to dull gray. I swallowed, grabbed the big shift lever, and clunked the transmission into gear. "Okay," I muttered to myself. "I'm ready if you are."

As if in response, a thunderclap blasted from the tailpipe. But I was moving forward now. I pointed the big chrome bumper at the empty road and started my long ride home.

CHAPTER 3

DRIVE ACROSS AMERICA twice in five weeks and you can't help but learn things.

I learned that the Rocky Mountains touch the sky, and the plains seem to stretch across forever. I learned that I don't mind driving alone. I learned that in Nevada, the temperature hovers at a nearly constant 350 degrees Fahrenheit. To live in Nevada is to live inside an atomic Easy-Bake oven.

Along with everything else, I learned that comfort is not something that the makers of the 1968 Chevrolet pickup truck really took into consideration when they built the thing. The vehicle was put together for butter-fed farm boys, not for skinny, cross-country runaways.

When Mom and I left Connecticut, we rarely drove more than two or three hours at a stretch. In fact Mom looked for any opportunity to pull off the highway. "Look," she'd say out of the blue. "Fresh eggs."

"What are we going to do with fresh eggs?"

"I just thought we'd stop and check it out."

By the time we crossed the Mississippi River, Mom didn't bother making up excuses. "Dulcie," she said, "my butt hurts."

In Wyoming, she dragged me into a tiny purple diner with a sign that said: Eat Here Get Gas. "How can we pass that?" Mom asked. The stop ended up with the two of us throwing up in a cheap motel outside Laramie. We took turns emptying our stomachs and rubbing wet cloths on each other's foreheads. "I thought Wyoming was cowboy country," Mom said, "not 'Land o' Food Poisoning.'"

"We've got to look more closely at those license plate mottos."

As I drove east by myself, I went over the things Mom and I had talked about on the road. "Why did we leave Newbury?" I asked her somewhere near Chicago.

Mom concentrated on the highway. "Can't we just enjoy this quality time together and not mess it up with conversation?"

"I've sulked for a thousand miles," I told her. "Even I'm bored with it."

She didn't say anything.

"Are you going to answer my question?" I asked.

Mom sighed. "Okay," she said. "I used to be the janitor's daughter."

Taunting my mother is a little like poking an animal in the zoo—never a truly good idea and definitely not recommended when you're in the cage too. Still, I couldn't resist. "So your life is a country-western song?"

"Do you want an answer or not?"

I nodded and tried not to grin.

"I fell in love with your dad, and then I became a janitor's wife." She paused, then turned to faced me. "That does sound like a country-western song."

"Yee-ha!" I said. "Watch the road."

Mom turned back toward the highway. "Maybe we should go to Nashville."

I shook my head. "I don't think so."

"We could be big stars," Mom said, "the next mother-daughter sensation."

"Except we can't sing."

"Nobody knows that, Dulcie. Until they find out, we could be anybody we want to be. If we stay in Newbury, I'll just evolve from janitor's wife into janitor's widow."

"You can't define people like that," I said.

"Of course you can." Mom turned to face me

again. "And janitor's widow is not what I want to be for the rest of my days."

"Watch the road!" I shouted.

Mom swerved back into our lane. "Listen," she said. "Leaving Newbury gives us a chance to define ourselves."

"I don't need to define myself."

"If you don't do it, somebody else will do it for you," said Mom.

"I know who I am," I said.

"You asked the question," Mom replied. "That's my answer."

"It's not a very good answer."

Mom gritted her teeth before she responded. "Dulcie," she said. "I'm doing my best."

I thought of a quote that Frank had posted on his office door. He and my father had covered the entrance to the Triple J janitor's office with Post-its and index cards that held poems, sayings, and, as Frank described them, assorted words of wisdom. "'When you drive away from everything you know,'" I recited from memory, "'you leave behind the mirrors that tell you who you are.'"

"Who said that?" Mom asked.

"I just did."

"I mean who said it first."

I shrugged. "I read it on Frank's office door."

"Dulcie," said Mom, "life is bigger than the janitor's door."

"Mom," I answered. "It's a pretty big door."

CHAPTER 4

CROSSING OUT OF CALIFORNIA, I drove through the Sierras, survived Nevada, and got halfway across Utah before I finally decided to give my mother a call. I stopped at a mini-mart that looked like an Old West saloon, and pumped quarters into an old-fashioned phone booth. I pulled the receiver away from my head before Mom answered. I wanted to protect the little bones in my inner ear from the screaming.

"Where are you?" Mom shouted.

"Green River," I said. "It's in Utah."

"How did you get there?"

"I took a wrong turn at Salt Lake City."

"Not funny, Dulcie."

"I'm not kidding," I said. "I really took a wrong turn."

"Are you okay?"

From where I was standing, I could see a couple teenage boys in cowboy boots and Hollywood-style ten-gallon hats staging a fake shoot-out. They did it every fifteen minutes or so to entertain travelers who stopped off Interstate 70. I'd watched them three times before I'd finally built up the courage to dial Mom's number.

"I'm fine."

"Dulcie Morrigan Jones," Mom said. "Come home right now."

"Mom, did you hear me? I'm in Green River, Utah."

"I don't care if you're in Grand Central Station, you better turn that truck around."

She kept going, but I turned my attention to the gunfight in the parking lot. Black-hat kid shot the white-hat kid. White Hat clutched his chest and stumbled to his knees. He crawled forward a couple steps, stretched out his pistol, and popped the Black Hat cowboy with three quick shots.

"What's that sound?" Mom asked.

"It's a shoot-out."

"No more kidding around, Dulcie. Bring me back my truck."

Both cowboys flopped dead on the blacktop.

"It's not your truck," I hollered into the pay phone.

Everybody, even the dead cowboys, turned to look

at me. I shrugged. The thousand miles between me and my mother made me feel pretty brave. "It's not your truck," I repeated. "It's Dad's truck."

There was a pause on the line. "Okay," Mom finally said. "Put your father on the phone."

Silence.

"So it is my truck."

"Very funny."

"I never thought you were the sort of kid who would run away," she said.

"I'm not running away," I shot back. "It's not running away when you're going home."

"It's still grand theft auto when you do it in somebody else's vehicle," she yelled.

She had me there. I wondered if she'd actually report me to the police. Then I recalled her explaining to my father once how she dealt with phone calls from difficult customers. "Some conversations need to end before they begin," she told him.

No one's ever said my mother isn't a smart lady.

"Mom," I said, "I'll call you from Newbury." I imagined her standing in the apartment staring at her beautiful view. Then I hung up.

If I'd had siblings or pets in the apartment with my mother at that moment, I would have had to fear for their safety. Thankfully, I had none.

I stepped over the cowboy in the parking lot and willed myself to calm down. Inside the Green River mini-mart, I picked up a bunch of bananas, a bag of pretzels, and a two-liter bottle of generic soda. Near the register, homemade apple pies sat beside a spindly wire rack filled with postcards. The pies looked fresh and good, so I pushed one toward the cashier. I spun the postcard rack around and noticed a few Old West scenes. There were horses, cowboys, and a couple proud Indians. I added stamps and the Western cards to my purchase and brought the whole load to the truck.

I forgot to pick up a plastic fork, so I sat on the back bumper and used my hands to scoop big bites of pie into my mouth. It was as good as it looked. When I finished, I wiped my fingers in the grass, dug a pen out of the glove compartment, and rested the postcards on my knee. I wanted to scratch a couple simple messages, one for Frank and one for Mom.

I glanced at the scrappy Utah landscape that surrounded me, and I couldn't think of a thing to say. Out of nowhere, I thought of my father and my grandfather working together on Dad's pickup truck. I remembered them standing in the auto shop looking over the torn-down pieces of the Chevy's big engine. Every nut, every bolt, every part was spread out across the floor like some kind of impossible jigsaw puzzle. Dad was shaking his head. Frank laughed out loud. He said, "It looks like we've reached the part of the project often referred to in technical terms as the what-the-hell-have-we-done moment."

Dad poked at the engine block with his toe and gave a little laugh. "That's the right question."

"No," said Frank. "Not really. The right question is, What are we going to do next?"

I took a breath of Utah desert air and felt myself floundering in my own what-the-hell-have-I-done moment. Sitting in that parking lot, I wasn't sure whether I was the engine or the mechanic, whether I was fixing things or breaking them. I wasn't even sure if I was running toward home or away.

I looked up to the sky thinking maybe I could find some sign, some signal from Dad in the Utah heavens. Instead, I found three huge turkey vultures circling overhead.

I patted the Chevy's bumper. "Don't worry," I said. "You're not edible."

The sun made my eyes water. I pretended like I wasn't crying. I thought about the huge expanse of road ahead. The driving didn't worry me, but three thousand miles was a long way to go, and I was less than a third of the way there.

I remembered something my grandfather said once. He and I were in his old station wagon. We were driving down Burlington Pike, a long, winding country road outside Newbury. We were going thirty-five miles per hour, just like the signs said, but cars roared up behind us and then flew past as soon as there was an opening ahead. "I swear," Frank said. "The last rebel in America is the guy driving the speed limit."

Maybe that's me, I thought. The last rebel in America. Seeing the U.S.A. in a Chevrolet at fifty-five miles an hour on her way home. I turned back to the postcards and wrote a simple list of words:

Home run.

Home stretch.

Home town.

Home free.

It looked like a little poem. Not much rhyme, but I think I'm more of a free verse girl anyway. I added one more line to the bottom:

Dulcie Morrigan Jones is almost home.

I liked that. I stamped the cards and dropped

them into the mailbox at the edge of the parking lot. I gathered the rest of my things together and scrambled back into the cab. I started the big engine and pulled back toward the highway. On the road, I found music on the radio. I sang along a little. I drove a lot, and I didn't cry some more.

CHAPTER 5

BY THE TIME I passed the Welcome to Connecticut sign, my backside felt like I'd been spanked from sea to shining sea. Mom would probably say I deserved it.

I spent an extra half hour cruising the back roads that led into Newbury. I could have stayed on the interstate, but I was cranky and sick of gray highway pavement.

I crossed through the downtowns of Thomaston and Plymouth and Bristol. I stopped at a little gift shop and picked up one last postcard, a field full of autumn ripe pumpkins, for Mom. I didn't write anything on the postcard except Mom's San Leandro address. I figured she'd know who it was from. A few more miles brought me to the John Jacob Jerome driveway.

Even before I parked the truck, I could see that the Triple J looked good. A school building in the summer is like a ship in a dry dock. Between June and September, everything got tuned up, tightened up, prettied up, and generally put back together. All of that happened under the direction of my grandfather.

The school's doors and window trim had been repainted. The grounds were green and neat. Around the entryway, bright splashes of white, orange, and yellow flowers were in bloom.

As I rolled down the driveway, I resisted the temptation to scream and shout and lean on the horn to announce my arrival. Instead I took a deep breath. I drank in the warm breeze that filled the truck with the wet green smell of cut grass, the keen and whine of summer cicadas. I was stiff and sore and tired of tires and engines and roads thrumming in my ears, but that was behind me now. I was finally back, and I couldn't wait to see my grandfather.

I let the truck glide into the empty parking spot marked Reserved for Principal, and before the engine stopped turning, I pushed my door open like an astronaut desperate to exit her tiny space capsule. "One small step for girl," I said to no one in particular.

I hopped down from the seat, steadied myself for a moment, then promptly toppled to the ground. My legs and back had cramped up after the brief postcard stop. I crawled to my feet and leaned both hands on the Chevy's big red fender.

"Hey," a voice called out. "Where'd you get that truck?"

I turned my head without standing upright. A tall, lanky girl stood ankle-deep in one of the flower beds that border the Triple J. She had a hoe in one hand and a small green trowel in the other. She wore a pair of faded blue jeans, a Red Sox cap, and a white T-shirt that said: I'M ALL LOST IN THE SUPERMARKET.

"You work here?" I asked.

"No." She pushed hair out of her face. It was red, the kind of dark red that almost looks black on a cloudy day. She stepped toward me. "I was just walking by," she said. "I noticed all the weeds in the flower beds around here, and I thought I'd clean the place up a little. Then I'll move on to the next town."

"Oh," I said.

"That's what I do," she said. "Weed. Move on. Weed. Move on."

"Okay." I struggled to an upright position. "That's nice. Have you seen Frank Morrigan?"

"Who wants to know?"

"He's my grandfather."

The girl took a closer look at me. "Are you Dulcie?"

"Yes."

She smiled. "We've been waiting for you." She dropped the hoe and stuck out a dirty hand. I took it.

"Hi," I said. "Who are you?"

"I'm Roxanne Soule. I work for your grandfather."

"You do?"

"You didn't really think I was the Johnny Appleseed of weeding, did you?"

I shrugged. "You never know."

"I'm not."

"Thanks for clearing that up." I took another look at her face. "I thought I knew everybody that worked here. I don't remember you."

"I'm new," she said. "Frank gave me the job after you left. I asked your dad for a job before that, but then, you know, he died."

"I heard," I said.

"You were a sophomore last year, weren't you?"

"That's right."

"I'm going to be a senior," said Roxanne.

"You still don't look familiar."

She smiled again. "I skip a lot of days. Nice to finally meet you."

"Thanks," I said. "Have you seen Frank?"

"He went to get his mail at the post office. Then

lunch and errands at home. Want to go surprise him?"

Frank's house was only a short ride away, but I really didn't want to get back into the truck. The inside smelled like fast food wrappers and stale coffee. There was a banana peel in there that I'd dropped beneath my feet somewhere in Pennsylvania, and the seats were sticky with donut crumbs and assorted spills.

"He's been waiting to see you," Roxanne went on. "He's been saying you'd be here any day now."

"You think he'll be back soon?" I asked.

"I don't know."

I looked around the school campus for a moment. Sleepy morning glories hung from a newly painted trellis near the front door. The flowers in the beds where Roxanne had been working were all the colors in a new box of crayons. They smelled good too. I glanced up at the polished blue sky. "Maybe I'll just wait here for him."

"Long ride, huh?" asked Roxanne. She didn't move from her spot.

"Not so bad."

"You want me to drive you to Frank's?" Roxanne asked.

"No," I said. "Really. I'll wait."

Roxanne looked uncomfortable.

"What?" I finally asked.

"Well . . ." She looked at the big Chevy. "You should move your truck."

"It's okay where it is."

"Didn't that used to be your dad's truck?"

"So?"

Roxanne pointed at the Reserved for Principal sign. "You should move it."

I laughed. "Mr. Bricker won't mind. He and Dad graduated from the Triple J together about a million years ago. Dad used to take his spot all the time."

Roxanne frowned. "I've heard Mr. Bricker tell stories about your dad. Weren't they friends?"

I nodded. Despite the difference in their job descriptions, Dad and Mr. Bricker had always been close.

"If Mr. Bricker pulled in right now," Roxanne went on, "he'd see your truck. I bet he'd recognize it, and for just a second he'd forget that your dad is gone."

I didn't say anything.

"Then he'd remember," Roxanne continued. "That would hurt. You would give him hope, and then you'd crush him like a bug." She waved the green trowel at me. "Never use hope to hurt someone."

"Is that some sort of rule?"

"It should be." Roxanne pointed at the truck. "Toss me the keys, and let's go see Frank."

I hesitated. For just a moment I wanted to resist, but then, for no good reason, I simply decided to trust this odd, bossy, weed-pulling girl.

Roxanne opened the door for me. "Hop in."

I climbed into the passenger seat. "You really think Frank is going to be happy to see me?"

"Are you crazy?"

"Do you think I'm crazy?"

"Why would I think that?"

"People don't run away from California to come to Connecticut," I said. "They usually go the other way around."

"You already tried the other way around," said Roxanne. "Everybody's allowed a do-over now and then."

"I'm just worried what Frank's going to say."

"Like maybe you drove thousands and thousands of miles just to get back to where you started?"

I shrugged.

"All that driving and now you're back at the starting line."

"Thanks," I said.

"I don't think that's what you've done."

I handed Roxanne the keys. "But I am back at the starting line."

Roxanne settled in beside me. She was taller than me, so she adjusted the seat and the mirrors before turning the key in the ignition. "People move the lines," she said. "I doubt this is the same place it was when you left. I doubt you're the same person you were when you left."

She gave the truck a little too much gas, and we leaped out of Mr. Bricker's parking spot.

"Easy there," I said.

Roxanne grinned. "I'm not the best driver in the world."

"Tell me that after we arrive."

Bouncing through Newbury in the passenger side of Dad's Chevy was both strange and familiar. I gazed out the window as my town rolled past like a Discovery Channel documentary. I thought of the last time I rode in the truck with Dad. It was the last day he was alive, a pretty day like this one. We had been on the way to school. I sat between my parents, and Mom was continuing an argument that she and Dad started over breakfast. "I don't care what you say,"

Mom insisted. "John Lennon is the most talented Beatle."

"You are wrong," said Dad.

Mom turned to me. "What do you think, Dulcie?"

"Aren't they all dead?"

"What does that matter?" asked Dad. He pulled the truck to a stop in front of Newbury Beauty, where Mom worked.

"It makes it a little hard to play a musical instrument."

"John and George are dead," said Mom.

Dad leaned across me and planted a kiss on Mom's forehead. "George lives. He was the best."

Mom pushed him away and slid out of the truck. "You don't know what you're talking about." She gave me a quick peck on the cheek and whispered, "I put a note inside his lunch bag. It says 'John Lennon rules.'"

I wondered what it would be like to have parents that acted like grown-ups.

"He put a note in your purse," I whispered back. "It says that if it wasn't for Yoko, John Lennon would be just an overrated pop star."

Mom stepped back toward the Chevy. "What's that supposed to mean?"

"Who's Yoko?" I asked.

"John Lennon's wife," said Mom.

Dad smiled. "Behind every great man, there's a great woman."

"You're lucky," Mom told him.

"Why's that?" asked Dad.

I gave my father a grin. "Because she loves you," I said. "Yeah, yeah, yeah."

Just then, the truck jerked to a stop. I looked up. I was surprised to see Roxanne Soule beside me.

"Dulcie," she said. "Welcome home."

CHAPTER 6

FRANK'S HOUSE looked like it had been drawn by a kindergartner with only two crayons, lime green and sunflower. The house used to be a rich, dark purple, but Frank changed it when the neighbors complained. "If they whine again," he warned, "I'm going to paint it like a Florida orange."

As I stepped out of the truck, it struck me that I'd been away from Connecticut for just a few weeks, but somehow I'd become unaccustomed to the color green. It was so little a part of the dry California landscape, but in Newbury it was everywhere. Frank's green house, green grass, green leafy trees—it was like swimming in green.

"Dulcie, is that you?" My grandfather's giant voice came down from above like thunder. Roxanne and I both looked up. "It's the prodigal granddaughter," Frank yelled from a perch near the peak of his steep roof.

"You're the prodigious one," Roxanne said.

"That's true," said Frank.

"What are you doing up there?" I asked.

Frank smiled and pointed at a huge copper pig balanced on a cast iron rod. "How do you like it?"

"You put a pig on the roof?"

"It's a weather vane," said Frank. "It's a well-known fact that pigs are sensitive to meteorological changes."

"Is he telling the truth?" Roxanne asked me.

"I have no idea," I admitted.

My grandfather is not a small man, and the extension ladder squeaked and moaned as he climbed down from the roof. Once safely on the ground, he yanked on a long gray rope and the ladder slid to half its size.

"Give me a hand, girls."

He lifted the extension ladder and tipped it toward the ground. Roxanne and I each grabbed the side rail and then followed Frank into the garage, where the light was dim and cool. We placed the ladder onto a couple pegs that stuck out from wooden beams along the wall.

In Frank's garage, just like in the rest of his house, everything sat in neat rows and assigned spaces. The orderliness of the place was sort of calming. It made me think of the way I kept things inside my head. Phone numbers, dates, memories, even people, everything has a place in there.

Whenever I thought of people, I pictured them just where I saw them last. In my mind, Dad was usually lying in a box, a nice box as far as boxes go—polished oak, brass fittings, and woodwork that Dad would be proud to call his own—but just the same, I'd prefer that he wasn't in it. Mom stood on her pretty patio admiring the San Francisco Bay.

For my grandfather, the last time I saw him he was giving me a hug and reminding me that I always had a home in Newbury. I had held that image of Frank in my head for weeks and weeks. Now I was standing back in my hometown worried that maybe Frank only meant it in the hypothetical sense, not in the sense of having your teenage granddaughter show up on your doorstep ready to move into the spare bedroom.

"So," Roxanne said to Frank. "Nice pig you put up there. What does it do?"

"I told you," said Frank. "He's a weather vane. He tells which way the wind is blowing."

"Which way is the wind blowing today?" Roxanne asked.

Frank wiped his hands on the back of his blue

workpants. "It seems to me," he said, "that the wind is blowing from west to east today, Roxanne." Then he turned to me and gave me a big smile. Before I knew what was happening, he wrapped me up inside a huge Frank Morrigan hug. "And look what the wind blew in," Frank said. "Just look what the wind blew in."

CHAPTER 7

AFTER I UNLOADED my few belongings from the truck, Frank and Roxanne ran back to the school to lock up for the day. By the time they returned, it was almost supper time, and Frank threw together one of my favorites, homemade macaroni and cheese.

"What are we going to do with you?" Frank asked me while we ate.

"Can we keep her?" said Roxanne. She'd stayed for supper.

"We might have to," said Frank. "If we send her back to California, her mother will kill her."

"I'm not going back," I said. "I'm staying here."

"That's not up to you," said Frank.

I felt my cheeks begin to burn red. "What do you mean?"

"Your mother's been in a panic for days," said Frank. "So have I."

"There was nothing to worry about."

Frank raised his eyebrows until his face looked like a big question mark. "You drove across North America all by yourself in a truck that was new before men walked on the moon. Your mom has been sitting by the phone expecting a ranger or a coyote to drag your bones out of a desert somewhere. Don't sit there and tell me there was nothing to worry about."

"I was on the highway," I said. "All I had to do was drive in a straight line."

"Your mother told me you got lost in Utah," said Frank.

I shrugged. "Just a little."

"You could have fallen asleep at the wheel. The truck could have broken down. Not to mention that you're just a—"

"If you say I'm just a girl, I'm going to back Dad's truck into your kitchen."

"I'll hold the door for you," said Roxanne.

"Something bad could have happened," Frank said.

"Nothing happened," I said.

"You could have hit a moose," said Roxanne.

"A what?" I asked.

Roxanne smiled a little. "A moose."

"Roxanne," said Frank. "I'll handle this."

"I didn't hit a moose," I said.

"Were you even looking?" she asked.

I bit my lip to keep from smiling. "No," I admitted.

"Well, then you're lucky."

Frank sighed. "I can't believe I'm going to put up with the both of you for the rest of the summer."

"So I can stay?" I asked.

Frank sighed again. "You can stay."

"I can stay!"

"But there are a few conditions," said Frank.

"Like heart conditions?" I asked.

"Like mental conditions," said Frank. "First, this is my house. If you live here, you follow my rules."

I nodded. I expected that.

"Second, you come back to work at the Triple J."

I barely hesitated. "Okay."

"But you don't get paid."

"What?"

"I have money for one student helper," said Frank. "Right now, I've got a pretty good one."

Roxanne gave me a sheepish smile.

"You could talk to Mr. Bricker," I said. "Maybe he has something left in his principal budget."

"Mr. Bricker probably would find the money to pay you, but I'm not going to ask him," said Frank.

"Why not?"

"You stole a truck and your mother's credit card," said Frank. "You really scared us. You've earned a punishment, Dulcie. You'll work without a paycheck until school starts. That's the deal."

"What if I don't accept?"

"Your mother sent me the title to the Chevy," he said. "I'll sell the truck tomorrow and use the money to buy you an airline ticket to San Francisco."

"I still owe Mom three hundred dollars."

"That's between you and your mother. And speaking of your mother, there's one more thing."

"What?"

"You have to call her."

I was quiet for a moment. "Can I think about that last one?"

"It's an all or nothing deal," said Frank.

"Take it! Take it!" Roxanne yelled. Frank and I both turned to stare at her in surprise. She smiled. "I love game shows."

"Well?" asked Frank.

I sighed. "I accept."

Roxanne started to clap. Frank put his hand on my shoulder. "It gives me great pleasure to welcome you back to the sacred guild of janitors," he said. "I hoped you would say yes."

"I didn't have much choice," I said.

"You always have a choice," said Frank.

"Janitor," I said. "A maintenance man or doorkeeper. Named after Janus, the Roman god of doorways and beginnings."

"That's stuck on the office door," said Roxanne. "That's us."

"It's only a partial definition," said Frank.

Roxanne lifted her lemonade. "Here's to the new janitor."

I raised my own glass. "Here's to new beginnings."

Frank met our glasses with his own. "Here's to doors."

Roxanne must have noticed my eyes closing. She drained her glass and pushed herself away from the table. "You should go to bed," she said. "I'll see you tomorrow. I want to hear about your trip."

I nodded. "Okay."

"Call your mother," Frank said just after Roxanne left.

"Do I really have to?"

"Janus would call his mother," said Frank.

I recalled the picture of Janus that Frank had taped to the door of the custodian's office. Like any good janitor, Janus was shown carrying a key. Unlike anybody on the Triple J staff, though, Janus had two heads. One always faced forward, the other always faced back. "That Janus doesn't know whether he's coming or going," I said.

"He's doing both," said Frank. "That's why he's god of beginnings. You always leave something behind when you start something new." Frank collected dinner plates and glasses to wash in the sink. "If I remember," he continued, "Janus didn't start out as a god. He started out as a mortal."

"But then he called his mother?"

Frank turned on the hot water. "He must have done something right."

I glanced at the clock. In California, it was barely six p.m. Mom was still at work. I took Frank's phone, punched in the apartment number, and at the sound of the beep said, "Mom, it's Dulcie. I'm with Frank. I'm home." Then, click.

Frank sighed. "Okay," he said. "It's a start."

CHAPTER 8

WHEN I WOKE UP, Frank was still snoring down the hall. It was earlier than I thought. I tiptoed downstairs and considered breakfast. My grandfather has been eating the same breakfast since forever. Cornflakes with milk plus a handful of raisins and several gallons of black coffee. I really don't know how he spooned that mush down. I scribbled a quick note.

> *Frank—*
> *I'll meet you at the kingdom.*
> *Love, DMJ*

The kingdom was the Triple J. Frank liked to stroll up and down the halls waving a plunger around his head like a scepter. He used to point the plunger at Dad. "One day this kingdom will be yours to rule," Frank would holler. "Rule it well, my boy. Rule it well."

"Is that a dagger I see before me?" Dad would cry.

"It's a plunger," Frank told him. "You need to get those eyes checked."

I grabbed my keys and slipped outside. It was still cool in the shade, but the sun was brilliant. A hot day was definitely in the cards. "Going to be a golly-whomper," I said out loud. That's what Mr. Bricker told us when big weather was on the way.

The red Chevy started right up. I backed the truck out of the driveway and turned left up Woodland Street. I felt my stomach drop a little as I crested the steep hill. Newbury is laid out like a deep cereal bowl placed upside down inside a large, shallow soup dish. Frank lived near the center of town, so almost every-where was a steep rise or a steep drop from his house.

I took a right-hand turn and cruised through a couple neighborhoods. I had plenty of time, and I enjoyed the feeling of knowing where all the roads go.

Both my parents were born in Newbury. My grandparents and their parents too. When Newbury first got put together, probably a few of my ancestors chopped down trees, planted the corn, or even dug the first outhouses. Somebody had to do it.

Eventually, Newbury became a factory town. It used to be the place to go if you wanted something pressed out of metal. A little museum inside

Newbury's city hall showed things that were made here: bicycle fenders, pie plates, milk cans, even tin soldiers and World War I army helmets.

As I rolled through the morning streets, I could see joggers and dog walkers and people carrying cups of coffee to their cars. I had to admit that Newbury folks looked a lot like the ones I'd seen in Wyoming and Ohio and Indiana and all across America. Those other places were friendly enough and pretty too, but I felt alone there. Apart. Here, even the air felt like a favorite shirt or well-worn shoes. Things fit me. I guess Dorothy was right when she told the Wizard of Oz: "There's no place like home."

Not that I'm a big Oz fan. To tell the truth, that movie scares me. Flying monkeys, crystal balls, midgets with lollipops, and that little dog too. It all sort of gives me the creeps. As a matter of fact, I made it across Kansas without sending even one wonderful wizard postcard to Mom. Instead, she received a card featuring Cappy the goat. That's Cappy as in capricious, as in impulsive and unpredictable, qualities I think my mother could appreciate. And Cappy the goat was not just any goat. Cappy was a fainting goat, a goat that—you guessed it—faints.

Really.

I found a flyer about fainting goats at a rest stop outside Wakeeney, Kansas. Come see the Kansas Fainting Goat Farm, it said. The goats looked sort of cuddly in the pictures, and even though the farm was a fair distance out of the way, I thought what the heck. A fainting goat is not something you see every day.

It took me a couple hours, but after some twists and turns I found a pretty little farmhouse, a red-painted barn, and a set of small corrals filled with real-life, honest to goodness, step right up and see 'em, fainting goats.

I didn't see anybody when I first arrived, so I parked the truck and walked over to a small corral near the barn. The goats, black and white and gray, wandered harmlessly around the pen. They seemed normal enough. According to what I'd read, a fainting goat is a slightly smaller version of a regular goat. Because of some weird genetic condition, though, a good scare caused them to pass out. Standing beside them, it seemed a little mean to scare them just for fun.

"Hey," I said to the goats.

"Hey, yourself."

That took me by surprise. There was nothing in the pamphlet that suggested that the goats could talk. "Who said that?" I called to the herd.

"Over here," said the voice. A big woman in overalls had her back pressed against the barn where the goats couldn't see her.

"What are you doing?" I asked.

"Don't you want to see 'em faint?" she asked in a stage whisper.

"Don't scare them," I whispered back.

"You gotta scare 'em." Before I could speak again, the woman jumped into view, leaped onto the top rail of the corral fence, and shouted, "HEY GOATS!"

Immediately, four of the small creatures toppled over. The rest made a mad, stumbling dash to the opposite side of the pen. As graceful as a gymnast, the woman hopped from the fence rail into the corral. "That's the way you do it," she said.

She quickly knelt down beside the supine goats and gently stroked their heads. "It's like a startle reflex," she said. "Their muscles just freeze up and they fall over. It doesn't hurt them."

"They could bump their heads when they fall," I said.

She laughed. "Goats have pretty hard heads." She smiled down at the animals. In a moment, the creatures were up on their feet and wandering around the corral again. "Shepherds used to keep fainting goats with their flocks as a sort of insurance policy against wolves."

"Let me guess," I said. "The goats head-butted the wolves away."

She shook her head. "If wolves attacked the flock, the goats got scared. They'd faint, and then they'd become wolf snacks. That would buy the sheep and shepherds enough time to get to safety."

"That's not fair," I said.

"The sheep never complained."

"What do the goats say?"

"The goats say maa-maa-maaa, and then they pass out." The woman wiped her hands on her pants. "They don't have to worry here," she said. "We just raise them because they're cute."

I watched the little animals milling around together. Bleating, butting heads, doing things that goats do, they looked like a bunch of grade-schoolers on a field trip. "They are cute," I agreed. "Do many people come to see them?"

"No, but the ones who do usually make the goats seem normal."

"What's that supposed to mean?"

"Who'd stop in Wakeeney just to see fainting goats?"

"Why else would you stop in Wakeeney?" I asked.

The farm lady grinned. "Good question."

"Do you have a gift shop?" I asked.

"What kind of tourist stop would this be without a gift shop?"

I followed the woman into the barn. One corner had been turned into a clean little store. I couldn't believe the number of goat-themed items that were available. I picked up the Cappy postcard for Mom and a fifty-cent sack filled with grain and dried fruit for the animals. Returning to the corral, I accidentally let the barn door slam behind me. Three more goats flopped to the ground. "Sorry," I said.

The animals recovered quickly, and I shared the snack. When they'd eaten all the food and tore the bag to shreds, I went back into the barn to say good-bye. The farm lady was gone, plowing the back forty or something. "Bye," I said to the empty room. "Watch out for wolves."

As I rolled away from the goat farm, the truck backfired. I'm sure the whole little herd went down. I stifled a laugh and thought of the Triple J hallways in between class periods, a hurricane of slamming lockers, kids shouting, bells ringing. Those goats would never survive in high school.

★　★　★

Even though the first day of school was still a couple months away, I was already a little scared myself. Driving around Newbury, I decided to mostly avoid my old friends and classmates for the summer. I wasn't ready to face the big deal they'd make over my recent tragedies and cross-country adventures. It was already clear, however, that I'd have to make an exception for Roxanne Soule.

I took another left on King Street and realized that I'd be driving past Roxanne's house. Frank told me where she lived the night before. I thought that Roxanne would probably be up by now, and maybe she'd like a ride to work. Maybe she'd like to get a donut. Maybe she just felt like some company. I know I did.

I found the address and pulled onto a gravel patch in front of a ratty-looking white house. The yard was mostly dead grass, and the sides of the house were stained black with some sort of mold. One window was missing a shutter. When I got out of the truck, a couple ugly cats darted away. The place smelled like a big litter box.

"Hey," somebody yelled from the house.

I'd been spotted.

It was Roxanne. She waved at me through an upstairs window and then disappeared. A moment later, she reappeared at the side of the house, stepping halfway through a screen door.

By stepping through, I mean that Roxanne actually peeled back the window screen from the inside of the frame and ducked her body through the metal rectangle.

"Come back here!" a voice yelled from inside.

Roxanne turned toward me. She had one foot on a cement stoop that stuck out from the side of the house. Her other leg was still inside the door. She smiled and gave another quick wave.

"That is a door!" a woman hollered. "Not an escape hatch!"

Roxanne stepped all the way outside and then turned back toward the door. "Mom," she said.

"Don't back talk me," the voice yelled. Through the screen, I could see a large woman. She grabbed the handle and shook the broken door.

"I'm sorry," said Roxanne. She backed away, and her mother gave the screen door a hard shove.

The door popped off its hinges and crashed out of its frame. Roxanne hopped out of the way. The screen door made a mad cartwheel past her and flipped into some scrubby bushes on the other side of the gravel driveway.

"Wow," I said under my breath.

The woman stepped into view. She was wearing faded blue sweatpants and a purple T-shirt. Her hair, long and limp, was the same burnt-red color as Roxanne's. It flew around her head and shoulders like snakes that had maybe been tortured by those cats I'd seen. Roxanne took another step back. For some reason, I thought of one of Frank's favorite pieces of advice. "When you don't know what's going on," he always said, "that's when you've got to take charge."

"Hey!" I said, way too cheerful. "You ready for work?"

Roxanne and her mother turned to me. Mrs. Soule's mouth squeezed shut in an angry line. Roxanne's eyes were open big and wide like a rabbit watching an eighteen-wheeler roar around a blind corner.

"Who are you?" Mrs. Soule snapped at me.

I stuck out my hand out and walked toward Mrs. Soule. "Dulcie," I said. "Dulcie Jones. I work with Roxanne at the Triple J."

Mrs. Soule squinted a little. She had to take my hand or I was going to stick it into her chest. "You?"

she said. "You're the one with the dead dad. What a way to kill yourself."

"That was an accident," said Roxanne.

Mrs. Soule pulled her hand out of my mine. Now that my fingers were free, I wanted to reach out, grab this woman by the throat, and squeeze.

"Whatever," said Mrs. Soule. Before I could say anything else she went on. "I went to school with your dad."

"Then you must know my mom too."

"Yeah," she said.

The three of us stood there without saying anything for a minute.

"Roxanne and I can probably fix that door." I pointed at the frame. "Frank won't mind if we use some hardware from the Triple J."

"Frank?" Mrs. Soule asked.

"My grandfather," I said.

"Our boss," Roxanne added.

Mrs. Soule shot her daughter a nasty look. "Right," she said, putting it all together. "All you janitors," she said to me. "What a bunch of busy beavers." She turned away.

"Nice meeting you," I said.

She waved without turning around, then reached

for the screen door that wasn't there. Her hand found nothing. She squeezed it into an empty fist and retreated into the house.

I took a deep breath and waited until I was certain that Mrs. Soule was gone. I turned to face Roxanne. "Want a donut?"

"A donut?"

"You know. They're like tires, but they're smaller and you can eat them."

She nodded. "Okay."

I could feel myself shaking as I walked back toward the truck. I wanted to march into the Soules' ugly little house and crush that woman like a bug. I climbed into the cab and gripped the steering wheel until I calmed down.

"Sorry," Roxanne said.

"It's okay," I said. "I have a mother too."

"Is she like that?" Roxanne asked.

"No," I had to admit. "Not quite."

We didn't talk again until I parked the truck at the Donut Stop.

"Is your mom home all day?" I asked.

"No," said Roxanne. "She works."

"Let's fix that door while she's gone."

"Okay," said Roxanne. "Thanks."

"What does your mom do?"

Roxanne made a funny face. "She runs the customer service desk at Kmart."

I shot a quick glance at Roxanne. "Really?"

"She loves the customers," said Roxanne.

"I bet."

"She loves them roasted, toasted, or fried on a bun."

We both began to laugh, and in the middle of laughing, I realized that I liked this girl. I liked her very much. For the first time since Dad died, I felt a bright stab of unexpected happiness. Maybe it was the laughter. Maybe it was the fact that I was worried about somebody other than myself for a change. In any case, the surprise of it took my breath away. I leaned forward and pressed my head against the steering wheel.

"It's going to be hard to drive like that," said Roxanne.

"This is how I steer," I said. "I communicate with this vehicle telepathetically."

"What's today's telepathetic message?"

I closed my eyes as if I were concentrating. I tilted my head to look at Roxanne. "This vehicle says that it is good to have a friend."

Roxanne smiled. She patted the dashboard. "Good truck," she said. "Good truck."

CHAPTER 9

WE PICKED UP a bag of donuts to share with Frank, and Roxanne asked me questions about my drive while we headed toward the Triple J. "I've read that pioneers lined the wagon trails between Pennsylvania and California with gravestones. Did you see any?"

"No," I said. "But I believe it."

"Imagine going three thousand miles in one of those rickety covered wagons with your mother."

"I don't have to imagine it," I said.

"Was it bad?" asked Roxanne.

I thought of the woman I'd just met at Roxanne's house. "Not really. It would have been easier if we had air-conditioning."

Roxanne laughed. "I bet pioneer girls felt that way too."

I caught a quick glimpse of myself laughing in the rearview mirror. I'd never noticed how a smile made me look like my father.

"What was your favorite part of the trip?" Roxanne asked.

I told her about mountains and deserts and great S-shaped rivers that I'd crossed. I listed a few of my favorite place names—Chimney Rock, Winnemucca, Paradise Hill, Toadstool, Hope—and we talked about the weird way that just a few new words could make you feel far away from home.

I told Roxanne about museums. "There's a museum for everything," I said. "Cameras, coat hangers, kitchen appliances, slot machines, you name it. It's like you're not allowed to build a town in America unless you have something weird to show off on Main Street."

"You went to all those places?"

"Not all of them, but some I couldn't resist. The toilet seat museum, the lightbulb museum, the barbed wire museum—"

"Barbed wire?" asked Roxanne.

"Pressed metal?" I replied. Every Newbury kid visited the city hall displays in grade school.

"That's true."

One of my favorites was the Great American Museum of Custodial Safety. I saw a small advertisement for the place when I stopped to eat in a

Missouri diner. My waitress drew a little map on a napkin, and after a short drive, I found a small town with a painted brick building near the town square. A collection of old hardware signs was tacked to the outside wall of the building, so I parked the truck at the curb, walked up to the front door, and went inside.

Despite the summer heat, the temperature in the building was cool and comfortable. A gray-haired man sat behind an old-fashioned cash register. He looked up from a worn copy of *Hemmings Motor News*. "Howdy."

"Hi," I said.

"Can I help you?"

I looked around. "I'm looking for the museum."

"Museum?"

"The Great American Museum of Custodial Safety."

The man lowered his magazine. "How'd you hear about that?"

I told him the truth. "There was an ad on my menu."

The old man smiled and gestured at the shelves around him. "This is it."

"This is a hardware store," I said.

"It's a museum too," he said. "I'm one of the artifacts."

"Oh." I looked around the room more slowly this time. The place reminded me a little of Frank's workshop, and the old man was friendly enough. "Where's the museum part?"

"I told you," he said. "This is it. That ad you saw was just a gaff banner."

"A what?"

"Gaff banner," he said. "A banner promising a world of wonders and a plethora of famous attractions. It's a carnival term. You're not from around here, are you?"

"No."

"The Great American Museum of Custodial Safety is a sort of local joke. It's just for fun, a way to make people feel that a trip to the hardware store is something special."

I didn't say anything.

"Did you actually come out of your way just to see the Great American Museum of Custodial Safety?"

I nodded dumbly.

"Well," he said. "Nobody's ever done that before."

I walked around the little store for a moment. I turned to the man. "Do you have any postcards?"

Now it was his turn to look dumb.

"I want a postcard of the museum."

The old man reached beneath the counter and pulled out a Polaroid camera. "You'll have to make one of your own."

Roxanne laughed when I showed her the photos. I'd been keeping them in the truck's glove compartment. "Did you send one of these to a practitioner of custodial safety?" she asked.

I shook my head. "No."

"Why not?"

I shrugged. "I decided to keep them. They remind me of my dad."

"Wasn't he a poor practitioner of custodial safety?"

I stared at the picture of the little brick storefront. A burning pressure seemed to be growing inside my throat and behind my eyes. But if I just waited, I knew that the feeling, the sensation of tears not yet cried, would pass.

Roxanne tapped a finger against the photograph. "Maybe things would have been different if your dad shopped there."

I took a breath and forced a smile. "Maybe."

That first day back, Frank put Roxanne and me on

cafeteria gum duty. "Scraping pine tar off chairs and tables will get you back in the swing of things," he told us.

"Pine tar?" said Roxanne.

"Pine tar, sugar, food coloring, and a baseball card," said Frank. "Wrap it up and you've got gum."

"Where did you learn that?" Roxanne asked.

Frank nodded at me.

"Bubble gum museum," I said. "It's in Indiana. I sent him a postcard from there."

Frank handed us buckets, scrapers, and spray bottles with the words GUM-OFF printed on the side. "I'll be in the faculty lounge if you need me."

"We scrape gum and you get to lounge?" asked Roxanne.

"I get to replace the teachers' toilet. Want to trade?"

"What happened to the old toilet?" I asked.

"Crushed beneath weighty faculty posteriors," Frank said.

"We'll stick with gum," I said.

"Good choice," said Frank. He turned away and waved without looking back. "Find me if you need anything."

"Is there anything he can't fix?" Roxanne asked.

"I doubt it," I said.

"I'd love to turn him loose on my mother."

I laughed. "My mother blames me for her disorders."

"Mine too," said Roxanne. "I wonder sometimes if she started with a screw loose or if it really was the process of giving birth that started her down the road to the nuthouse."

I ducked beneath a cafeteria table to search for used gum. "You'll never believe the first place my mom made us stop when we got to California," I said.

"Where?"

"Donner Pass."

"What's Donner Pass?"

"It's where a group of pioneers, the Donner party, had to eat each other to stay alive. It happened in the eighteen hundreds. They tried to cross the mountains in winter, but they got stuck in the snow. They ran out of food and a bunch of them died."

"I guess you'll eat anything if you get hungry enough."

"I don't know about that."

Roxanne struggled with a nasty piece of gum stuck to the bottom of a folding chair. "Instead of the Donner party, they should have called it the dinner party."

"Very funny."

"Thank you." Roxanne popped the gum off the chair with a snap.

I found my own wad of Bazooka and started scraping. "My mother's favorite thing about the Donner party was that two-thirds of the women survived, but only a third of the men made it."

Roxanne stood up. "Your mother's right," she said.

"Right about what?"

Roxanne gave me a big grin. "Sometimes it's good to be a girl."

CHAPTER 10

THERE IS A RHYTHM to good work. As days turned to weeks, Frank tried to help us find that rhythm by turning the school public address system into something he called Custodial Forces Radio. "You get more than a paycheck when you work at the Triple J," Frank told Roxanne and me on a hot day in June.

"Good thing," I said, "since I don't get a paycheck."

"That's your own doing," Frank reminded me. "By the way, have you talked to your mother lately?"

"I call her," I said. "She's never home."

Frank raised an eyebrow. "In these halls," he continued, "you get a vibrant selection of rock and roll featuring every strand of the American musical tradition."

"I leave a message," I said, mostly to myself. I didn't add that I only called California when I knew Mom would be at work. "Nice messages," I added.

"Vibrant selection?" Roxanne said to Frank. "All you ever play is Elvis."

"Featuring every strand of the American musical tradition," said Frank. "Blues, country, gospel—"

"He's just trying to make us forget that we stick our arms in toilet water," I said.

Frank shrugged. "If you have to spend time cleaning the toilet, wouldn't you prefer to spend it with Elvis?"

"Elvis and his toilet were very close during his last moments on earth," I observed.

"Elvis and his toilet were seen boarding a Greyhound bus in New Haven last week," Roxanne added.

"Girls," said Frank. "The man is dead. How about a little respect?"

Roxanne gave my grandfather a grin. "R-e-s-p-e-c-t," she said. "Find out what it means to me."

Frank groaned. "First Elvis, now Aretha."

"You can hear God's voice when Aretha Franklin sings," Roxanne stated in a fair imitation of my grandfather.

"When Aretha sings, God knows that he better sit down, shut up, and listen," I said, doing my own impersonation of Frank.

Roxanne laughed out loud. Even Frank couldn't hold back a smile.

"Which is it?" Roxanne asked.

Frank reached into the supply closet and handed us each plastic gloves and clear plastic spray-bottles filled with blue liquid. "Girls," he said, "be thankful that you live in the kind of complex and beautiful universe that allows both those statements to be true at the same time. Now get to work."

"You have a bottle in there for everything," said Roxanne.

I held mine up to the window. The sunlight reflecting through the blue liquid was pretty. "Frank's secret money-saving window-washing formula," I said.

Roxanne opened her spray bottle and sniffed. She quickly crinkled up her nose and popped the cap back onto the container. "Vinegar?"

"Vinegar and blue food coloring," said Frank. "I mix it up so it looks just like the stuff you'd buy at the store."

"Vinegar cleans windows?" asked Roxanne.

"It's better than ammonia and cheaper too." Frank handed us buckets, rags, and two small squeegees. "You know what to do."

"I hate windows," I muttered to Roxanne.

"Sorry," she said.

It was a beautiful sunny day, and we could have been working outside except that Roxanne had come to work with Band-Aids wrapped around eight of her fingers.

"What happened?" Frank asked her.

"I dropped an iron," she said.

"On your hands?"

"I tried to catch it."

"It looks like you succeeded."

Roxanne shrugged. "I guess I did."

"No weeding for you," said Frank.

We sprayed and wiped, and I let my mind wander. I thought about working with my dad. He and I had a favorite conversation, a sort of ongoing debate about how movies work. How they tell stories. The most important part of our conversation concerned who we would choose to play all the parts in the never-to-be-released blockbuster, *The History of Newbury*.

"Who do you think should play God?" Dad asked me once.

"God is going to be in *The History of Newbury*?"

"Sure," said Dad.

He was smiling, but I could tell he was really

curious about my answer. I remembered that we'd watched Dad's favorite movie, *Star Wars,* for about the millionth time the night before. "How about James Earl Jones?" I asked. He was the voice of Darth Vader.

"You think a big voice is enough to play God?" Dad asked.

"Then Marlon Brando," I said.

"Which Brando?" Dad asked. "*On the Waterfront* Brando? *Apocalypse Now.* Brando? *Godfather* Brando?"

"All of them. That's why he's perfect."

Dad nodded. "Good answer."

"What about you?" I asked. "Who do you want to play the part?"

"James Earl Jones," he said.

"No fair!"

"Okay," he said, thinking about it for a moment. "Maybe we could work God's name into the title and then try to convince him to make a cameo appearance as himself."

"Better be careful," I said. "Maybe God is a she."

He laughed. "I wouldn't be surprised."

Thinking about the movie, I realized my cast of characters was changing. I decided that Mom, Dad,

Frank, and now Roxanne should all play themselves. An unconventional choice, I know, but the critics would rave.

"I smell like a pickle," Roxanne announced.

I turned to look at her. She had on a Triple-J Falcons T-shirt that was three sizes too big. She was wiping down windows with just her palms. She'd sprayed too much vinegar on the glass, and the fingers on both her hands were splayed up like she was a baby lizard trying to crawl across sand that was way too hot.

"Roxanne," I asked. "Were you born in Newbury?"

"Oh, sure," she said.

"And you really did know my dad?"

"Yup."

I polished the window in front of me. "I thought I knew everything about him," I said. "But he never mentioned you."

"You don't believe me?"

"I believe you. I'm just trying to figure things out. I mean, who are you? Where did you come from?"

Roxanne gave me a strange grin. "Those are good questions. I wonder about them all the time. Don't you?"

CHAPTER 11

JUNE AND JULY washed away inside John Jacob Jerome beneath a shower of floor wax, blue vinegar, and rock and roll oldies. I welcomed August—the beginning of the end of summer—by cooking up a huge pan of *Facioli alla sutrina,* an Italian recipe for steak and beans. Roxanne came over again. Frank explained that he'd extended an open invitation to Roxanne right after he hired her. "Her mother works a lot," said Frank. "If I didn't feed her, I think she'd eat nothing but crackers."

He didn't add that he hated eating alone.

Frank and I were sitting on the porch when Roxanne and her mom pulled up in an old Jeep. "Do you have time to come in?" Frank called to Mrs. Soule. "We have plenty."

"No," said Mrs. Soule. "I have to work."

"Maybe another time," said Frank.

Mrs. Soule paused. She looked as if she were

measuring Frank's words, testing them to see if they were true or if he was making fun of her. "Maybe," she said.

Roxanne stepped down from the Jeep. "Bye," she said to her mom.

"How's that door?" I called to Mrs. Soule. Roxanne and I had fixed their screen door earlier in the week.

Mrs. Soule revved the Jeep's engine. "It's fine," she said. Then she roared away.

"You're welcome!" I called after her.

"Don't let her get to you," said Roxanne. "She's upset."

"She's always upset," I said.

"She owes somebody money," said Roxanne. "She's going to give him her Jeep. We won't have a car after today."

"Do you want us to pick you up for work?" asked Frank.

"I can walk," said Roxanne. "It's not far."

"Let me know if you change your mind." Frank turned to the house. "Let's eat."

Roxanne and I followed Frank into the kitchen and took seats around the table. Meals at Frank's house always started with a prayer. Sometimes

Frank just hollered, *"Grazie,"* at the ceiling and then, "Let's eat!" Other times, Frank used mealtime as an opportunity to provide analysis, critique, and specific instructions to God so that the Almighty might do a better job of running the world. "Even the Lord can use some honest advice now and then," Frank said.

When we were settled, Frank said, "Dulcie's mom is going to say grace tonight."

"What?" I asked.

"Your mom," Frank said. "She left a prayer on the answering machine."

"You're kidding."

"Listen." Frank reached behind his chair and pushed a button on the phone.

"Hi, Dad." It was my mom's voice. "If God doesn't need a lecture today, maybe you could play this before your next meal. Tell Dulcie I miss her."

I raised my eyes in a question.

"Don't worry," Frank said. "This is good."

Mom's voice continued on the machine. "So there's this atheist swimming in the ocean." She sounded tinny and far away, like we were playing the message on an old wind-up phonograph. "The atheist sees a great white shark in the water, and the shark is

79

speeding toward him. The atheist starts swimming like crazy, but the shark is gaining. The atheist screams, 'Oh God! Oh God! Save me!'

"Suddenly, a bright light shines down from above and God yells, 'YOU'RE AN ATHEIST. WHY DO YOU CALL WHEN YOU DON'T EVEN BELIEVE IN ME?'

"The atheist knows he can't lie. 'It's true that I don't believe in you,' he says, 'but how about the shark? Can you make the shark believe in you?'

"'NO PROBLEM,' says God.

"Suddenly, the shark stops. It closes its eyes, bows its head, and says, 'Thank you, Lord, for this food I am about to receive.'"

Frank hit the stop button on the phone machine. "Amen!" he hollered. He and Roxanne began to laugh. "Let's eat."

"Is there any more?" I asked.

"That was it," said Frank.

"That was good," said Roxanne.

"What exactly was she trying to say?" I asked.

"Don't swim with atheists?" Roxanne suggested.

"She just wanted to make us laugh," said Frank.

"I don't know," I said.

Roxanne grinned and took a bite of her supper.

"Dulcie, this is delicious. Did your mother teach you to cook?"

I pointed at Frank. "The janitor taught me."

Frank held up his fork. "I didn't teach you this." He put the fork into his mouth. "I wish I did."

"I got the recipe from a nun in Ohio."

"Why are all nuns short?" asked Roxanne.

Frank looked up at the ceiling. "Oh, God, save me!"

"You're not an atheist," I said.

"I'm just praying that the lightning aimed at Roxanne doesn't accidentally hit me."

"The nun who gave me the recipe wasn't short," I said.

Roxanne shrugged. "Maybe nobody gave her the job description before she signed up."

CHAPTER 12

I HAD MET Sister Clare at the Shrine of the Holy Relics in Maria Stein, Ohio.

"Any cool stuff to see around here?" I'd asked the first gas station kid I met when I crossed into Ohio. My backside was so sore that day that I would have stopped to see fresh eggs.

"If you like bones," he said while the truck swallowed up gas, "you should go to Maria Stein."

"Who's Maria Stein?"

"Not who," he said. "Where. It's the name of a town."

"I never heard of a town with a first name and a last name."

"How about New York," the kid said. "Or Los Angeles?"

"What's in Maria Stein?"

"I told you," he said. "Bones. Lots and lots of bones. They're pieces of saints."

"How far is it?" I asked.

"Not too far. And it's cool."

The gas station attendant gave me directions and told me to look for the Convent of the Sisters of the Precious Blood. "And don't forget Salt Lake City," he yelled as I drove away. "That one has a middle name!"

If I ever have children, they will not go to public school in Ohio, but at least gasboy's directions were good. I followed his instructions all the way to Maria Stein, where I discovered the Shrine of the Holy Relics, home to over a thousand relics, some very fancy reliquaries, and a really pretty church.

According to the dictionary, a relic is an object kept for its association with the past, especially a piece of the body or a personal item of a saint. A reliquary is the fancy container used to hold relics. Why not just call them bones and boxes? I don't know.

When I arrived at the shrine, the place was mostly dead. I suppose a place like that is always mostly dead.

A tall woman stood up from behind a desk in the corner. "Welcome," she said. "I'm Sister Clare. I'm the docent here today."

I did not know what docent meant. I figured it was either a recruiter or a security guard, but she was actually more like a tour guide.

"Hi," I said. I glanced at the hundreds of containers around me. "Are these all bones?"

"No," said Sister Clare. "There's hair and teeth too, some fingers, a couple ears. I think we may have somebody's tongue."

"Oh, yuck."

Sister raised an eyebrow. "There's also jewelry, clothes, and assorted objects that saints may have used during their lifetimes."

"Wow," I said. "Can I look around?"

"Please do," said Sister Clare. "Just don't touch the relics."

"I wouldn't think of it."

I wandered around a little. A box holding a fragment of cloth said to be worn by Jesus' mother, Mary, was displayed prominently. There were bones and strands of hair from hundreds of former popes and bishops and martyrs. I couldn't help but notice that there were a lot of virgins too.

I felt a little bad for the virgins. Their status in that department—and mine too, for that matter—didn't bother me one way or the other, but who'd want it printed on top of their remains for all eternity?

"What's all this stuff doing in Ohio?" I asked.

Sister Clare relaxed a little, probably happy that I'd asked something that she could answer. "Our convent was established in the mid-1800s to serve German immigrants that were settling Ohio then. At the same time, there were wars in Europe. Catholic churches in Rome were being ransacked, and Church officials were concerned that the relics within them were in danger of being desecrated."

"So they sent them to Ohio?"

"Nobody was ransacking Ohio."

I walked around. I saw a golden crucifix that claimed to hold a splinter of Jesus' cross. Sister Clare found me looking at it.

"It is said that the hilt of Charlemagne's sword was made to contain two splinters from the true cross," she told me. "Personally, I believe that if you gathered all the known pieces of Jesus' cross in one place, you'd have enough wood to build an ark."

"You mean they're fake?" I asked.

"Some," she said. "Relics were a big business in the Middle Ages. There are three different medieval cathedrals built for three different true skulls of John the Baptist." She smiled. "It is safe to assume that at least two are not authentic."

"Then why keep them?"

"How to know which one is real?" She pointed at the golden reliquary. "That one may very well be from the cross that held Jesus."

I stared at the small crucifix. I turned to Sister Clare. "Whether it's fake or not, it's still just a chip of wood in there, isn't it?"

She paused and looked at me with something like surprise in her face. "I've often thought that myself." She turned to examine the little sliver within the crucifix. "It's strange the things we keep. I think it's our nature, our human nature, to rely on objects that we can touch and hold and feel. They help us to remember people and places, and moments that are important."

I nodded. "Touching something really does seem to make a difference."

"Yes," said Sister Clare. "I think so."

"But you can't touch anything here, huh?"

She laughed. "No. You can't."

I walked around a little more until I found something else interesting. "Hey," I said out loud. "What's this?"

I pointed at a modest reliquary. Sister Clare came and glanced over my shoulder. "Saint Dulcissima," she read aloud. "A virgin martyr known as the patron saint of Sutri, Italy. Why do you ask?"

"My name is Dulcie," I said.

"Ah," she said. "People often look for saints with whom they share a name. We have Saint Clare here too. She's the patron saint of television."

"There's a saint for television?"

"There's a saint for everything. Clare is also a patron of embroiderers, eye disease, and laundry workers, among other things."

"That Clare was a pretty busy lady."

"She was the daughter of a count and a countess. Her father died at a very young age. When she was a teenager, she met Saint Francis, and then she ran away from her mother's palace to follow the word of God."

"Is that when she got the eye disease?"

"I'm not sure about that," said Sister Clare.

"What do you know about Dulcissima?"

Sister Clare bent over to look more closely at the little card in front of Dulcissima's reliquary. "It doesn't look like much is known about her." She straightened up. "But I have visited the town of Sutri."

"In Italy?"

"Yes," said Sister Clare. "In Italy."

"Is Sutri famous for anything?" I asked.

Sister Clare laughed. "Sutri is famous for a local bean that does not give you gas."

"You're kidding."

"Sutri beans were well known even to the ancient Romans," said Sister Clare. "They built an amphitheater in Sutri that's still there, but if you ever visit, you should try to go during the bean festival."

"You're telling me that Saint Dulcissima is the patron saint of the no-fart bean."

"Oh, no," said Sister Clare. "Dulcissima is the patron saint of the town that produces the no-fart bean. The bean probably has a patron saint of its own."

I couldn't tell if she was kidding. "I'll look around and try to find him."

Sister Clare nodded. "I agree," she said with a perfectly straight face. "If beans have a patron saint, I am sure it is a man."

I was starting to like this woman.

I looked, but I didn't find Saint Cannellini or any other patron saint from the legume family. There were plenty of others, though. While I walked, I thought about what Sister Clare had said about memory and objects and things. I remembered a time that Mom, Dad, and I had gone to a baseball game. I caught a foul ball. It was a complete accident. I am not an athlete, but with that ball in my hand, I suddenly had a better sense of the game. I could feel long summers of playing catch in the backyard. I understood a little more about standing in the outfield, waiting to make a diving catch, all because I held that lace and leather in my palm.

Maybe that's why I wanted Dad's red truck, wanted to sit at my grandfather's kitchen table and look at the scratches in the Formica tabletop, why I held on to paperback books and worn dictionaries that Dad gave me. These things were my own relics—pieces and fragments of places and people that I could hold and remember. Maybe Mom could leave all that behind, maybe she even needed to, but I couldn't do that.

I sat on the floor of the shrine and stared at the light coming through the deep blue stained glass. I started to cry. I felt a hand on my shoulder. Sister Clare knelt down beside me. "Are you all right?" she asked.

I shrugged. "That whole bean thing," I said. "It was very upsetting."

Sister Clare laughed. "You are funny." She pulled a tissue from some hidden pocket and wiped my tears. "You are going to be okay."

"What makes you say that?"

"Laughter," said Sister Clare. "You don't get a good laugh from people who are moving toward despair."

"You don't?"

"Not if you're a nun."

I wiped my nose on my sleeve. "I guess you're right," I said. "I already passed Despair in Utah. I'm going to Newbury. That's in Connecticut."

She laughed again. Before I left, I purchased a really pretty postcard, one that showed the shrine's stained-glass windows. I asked Sister Clare to write something good on the back. She gave me the steak and beans recipe. "I learned this from the friends I made in Sutri," she said. "You're going to love it."

I read the recipe out loud to Frank and Roxanne. "*Facioli alla sutrina*: First fry a small piece of lard or fat with a chopped onion, add some peperoncino, a basil leaf, and a chopped stick of celery. Add beef slices or steaks. When the beef is cooked well enough, add chopped tomatoes and boiled Sutri beans. If you can't find Sutri beans, any bean that you like will do. Continue to cook until the juice has been reduced. Say a prayer of thanks and serve warm."

Frank raised his glass. "Amen."

CHAPTER 13

THE MORNING AFTER our dinner party was a Saturday, so I slept in a little. I came into the kitchen around eight. Frank had already finished his breakfast. "Cornflakes?" he asked.

"No," I said. "That's okay."

"Still full from last night?"

"Yes," I said. "That's it."

"How about we go for a ride?"

"Where to?"

"Let's go visit your grandmother," Frank said. "I'll drive."

I followed Frank to his station wagon. In ten minutes we were inside the Newbury Memorial Cemetery. I sat in the shadow of a small maple tree and watched my grandfather lie down on green grass as soft and thick as dog fur. "I don't know," he said out loud.

"What don't you know?" I asked.

Frank shifted from his backside onto his belly. "I don't know how I'm supposed to find a spot that will be comfortable for all eternity." Frank's head was just a couple inches away from a fat slab of rose-colored marble that was already etched with his name and birth date.

"Doesn't that stone creep you out a little?" I asked.

"Dulcie," he said, "that stone annoys me."

"Because it reminds you that you're going to die?" I asked.

"We're all going to die." Frank turned to face me. "And when it happens to me, I will be buried beneath this." He pointed at the stone. "Pink. Your grandmother just had to have a pink stone."

"It's rose," I said.

Frank shook his head. "Roses are red. That stone is pink."

My grandmother's name, Margaret Alma Morrigan, along with the dates of her birth and death rested solidly on the stone. She died before I was born, but you could still find her influence at Frank's house in the pink bathroom sinks and the pink tile on the kitchen counter. From the stories I've heard about my grandmother, I think she and I would have gotten along well.

"I tried to reason with her," said Frank. "I mean, we're talking about eternity here. What would have been wrong with white or gray?" He rolled onto his back again, closed his eyes, and shifted his body around on the grass. "I wonder if I can get a casket with lower back support."

"Oh sure," I said. "I bet you can get one with little speakers and a CD player too."

Frank sat up a little and raised his eyebrows.

"I'm joking," I said. "And anyway, you wouldn't be able to change the disc. What music could you listen to until the end of time?"

Frank smiled. "That's the sort of question that would have kept your dad and me busy for days."

Dad and Frank loved to throw crazy problems and challenges at each other. It was mostly Trivial Pursuit stuff, fuel for discussion while they worked. They spent hours deciding the best hitter in baseball (Ted Williams), the best Beatles album (*Rubber Soul*), the best U.S. President (Harry Truman), and a ton of other answers to earth-shatteringly unimportant questions.

There were times, though, that they'd turn their attention to more meaningful items: the best teacher at the Triple J (Mr. Ted Bricker, principal), the best course of study for Dulcie when she goes to college (undecided), the funniest word in the dictionary (*naugahyde* for Dad, *syzygy* for Frank, *wikepedia* for me. Something about the *W* cracks me up).

"When Gram picked the stone," I said, "did she know she was, you know . . . ?"

"Going to need it soon?"

I nodded.

"Your grandmother had cancer," Frank said simply. "She knew."

"So you couldn't really say no."

"When it came to your grandmother, I never mastered that particular skill." Frank smiled. "And anyway, she got such a kick out of buying the dumb thing."

We were both quiet for a little while.

"Mom said that I take after my grandmother," I finally said.

"You do," said Frank. "So did she."

"Does that mean I have to marry a janitor one day?"

Frank smiled. "Only if you're lucky. Let's go check on your dad."

It might sound weird, but I actually enjoyed walking through the cemetery with my grandfather. The names on the stones were comfortable and familiar. Kazmarczyk, Aiello, Laporte. Donahue. I went to school with kids from those families. My parents had too. So had my grandparents. "I recognize some of these people," I said.

"The older you get," said Frank, "the more dead people you know."

"You say that like it's a good thing."

"It is," said Frank. "It means they're dead, and you're not."

I stepped over a small stone marker above the graves of Mr. and Mrs. Eugene Villapondi. They used to give me slices of provolone cheese at their deli on Forest Street. Their son ran the place now. We walked by my first piano teacher, Ms. Nancy Dekow. Thanks for the gold stars, I thought. I said hi to the big stone above Mr. and Mrs. George Marsh. They used to be my grandfather's neighbors. I'd always wondered why my parents seemed a little intimidated by Mr. Marsh. He was a small, kind man. Then I'd learned he'd been the John Jacob Jerome principal when Mom and Dad were kids. I guess he wasn't so kind and gentle then.

"Why didn't we put Dad near you and Gram?" I asked.

"I'm not buried yet," Frank said.

"You know what I mean."

"You should never move right next door to your parents," Frank said. He stopped walking. "Here we are."

Dad's stone was the same speckled rose color as my grandmother's. Mom and I picked it out. Even in the middle of that terrible time, there was still something inside each of us hoping that another pink stone would be something to smile about one day.

Frank turned to face the headstone. "Years from now, people who knew your father and me will visit our graves. They'll stop and think about us. They'll think that we bought our stones at Bed, Bath and Beyond."

Mom and I dragged Frank into the mall one time before my freshman year at the Triple J. He still had not recovered.

"Caskets are in the Beyond section," I said. "We've preordered one for you that has little pockets in the lining for bath oil and potpourris. You'll smell really good when you meet St. Peter."

Frank rolled his eyes.

"Every little bit will help," I added.

"I'm making my own pine box," Frank said. "Just

stuff some Wrigley's spearmint into my armpit."

"Pine tar and sugar," I said. "That will be nice."

He leaned down into the grass at the front of Dad's headstone. "Sit," he said to me.

I parked myself beside Frank. I looked down at the grass and imagined the coffin beneath us. "Well," I said. "Now what?"

"Now nothing," said Frank. "We stay and visit your dad for a while."

I sat quietly for a moment. "You think he's really here?" I finally asked.

"I don't know where he is, Dulcie." Frank waved his hands at the headstone, the trees, the whole cemetery. "When I come here, I feel like your dad and your grandmother are not so far away. It's a nice place to come and talk with them once in a while."

"Do they talk back?"

"Sure," said Frank. "But not like ghosts. It's more that I know them so well that I know what they'd say if they were sitting here too."

"Sometimes I knew what Dad was going to say before he said it."

"Exactly," said Frank. He leaned back on the grass and closed his eyes. "Sometimes I come just because it's a nice place to take a nap."

I looked around the cemetery. The rows of stones across the green grass and the thought of all the dead bodies beneath me made me feel a little queasy. But I liked the big trees that surrounded the place. Their leaves and branches moved in the wind like huge arms and long hair. It didn't make me think of ghosts or spirits or anything like that. Instead, the trees swayed green and loose like giant undersea animals. They made me feel like some tiny fish or microscopic plankton pushed around by invisible currents.

I reached out and put my hand on the pink marble with my dad's name on it. I wanted to feel something back from that stone. It was cold and smooth, but I wanted something else, something immediate and strong.

I closed my eyes and took my hand away from the gravestone. All I really felt was tired. Hungry too. I should have eaten those cornflakes. I should have done a lot of things. I went to rest my arm at my side, but I brushed against Frank. He reached out his hand, rough with work and calluses. He found my fingers and squeezed.

I opened my eyes and stared at my grandfather on the grass beside me. I had not cried in a while, but sometimes a quick sniffle or a brief sob would sneak up on me without warning.

"Sometimes," I whispered, "I feel very breakable."

Frank did not open his eyes. "Sometimes we notice that we are human," he said. "That is not always a pleasant feeling."

CHAPTER 14

I DIALED THE PHONE and listened to it ring. When the machine at the other end beeped, I began to speak. "Hi, Mom. It's Dulcie."

Since I'd been back in Newbury, I'd only had to talk to my mother a couple times. The few times she'd been home to pick up, I'd said a quick hello, then passed the phone straight to Frank. I took a breath and started to speak again. "I visited Dad today. It was—"

"Dulcie," Mom's voice interrupted me. "Dulcie, it's me."

"Mom," I said, surprised. "What are you doing there?"

"I live here."

"I mean—"

"I know what you mean. I took a day off. I'm just hanging out on the patio."

"Oh," I said. "How's the view?"

"Great," she said. "A little lonely."

There was an awkward silence. I wanted to say things to her, but I was out of practice. Plus, I was afraid of what she might say back.

"How are you?" Mom asked.

"Fine."

"Good," said Mom.

More silence.

"I want to tell you that I liked all those postcards," said Mom.

"Yeah?"

"Send me some more."

"I haven't gone anywhere lately."

"That's okay," she said.

"Frank says he's going to take me and Roxanne to the ocean next week," I said. "I could send you a postcard from there."

"I've seen the ocean," said Mom. "Send me something from where you are right now."

"Right Now is a town in Nevada," I said. "It might take me a while to get there."

"Dulcie," said Mom. "I don't care where the postcards are from. It's who they're from that matters."

I didn't answer.

"So you visited your dad?" said Mom.

"Sort of," I said.

"How was that?"

"He's still dead."

Mom didn't answer.

"I'm sorry," I said. "It wasn't bad. The cemetery is pretty. Like a park."

"A park," said Mom. "I never thought of it like that." She sounded tired and maybe a little annoyed.

I realized then that I wanted to see my mom. I couldn't tell exactly what we were talking about on the phone sometimes. A face-to-face conversation would be a lot better. Still, we tried to make small talk. I told Mom a little more about Roxanne.

"Your dad talked about Roxanne," Mom said. "He wanted to help her. Does she still live with her mother?"

"Yes," I said. "Why?"

"Your father and I went to school with Roxanne's mother."

"That's what Mrs. Soule told me."

"You've met her?" Mom asked.

I told her about the few times we'd crossed paths.

"I'd prefer that you stay clear of her, Dulcie."

"Why?"

"Roxanne sounds very nice," Mom said. "But even when her mother was a kid, she was not . . ."

She paused. "Just before we left Newbury, your dad was concerned that Francine Soule had become a pretty rotten adult. He was really worried about Roxanne."

"I see Roxanne almost every day," I said. "Frank keeps an eye on both of us."

"That's good," said Mom. "I hear you're donating your time to the Triple J."

"Thanks to you," I said.

"No," said Mom. "That was your doing."

"Now I'm John Jacob Jerome's custodial slave."

"You're more like an indentured servant," said Mom. "It could be a lot worse."

A few weeks earlier, I would have come back with some smart-mouth reply. I knew how to make Mom angry in a flash, and sometimes I liked doing it just because I could. Now I was starting to think that maybe the rough treatment she and I had gotten into the habit of giving each other didn't have so much to do with her and me. Maybe it was the dead guy we were mad at.

"It's good to talk to you, Dulcie," Mom said after a long silence. "I miss you."

"I miss you too."

We hung up, and I spent a few moments dissecting

the conversation. We'd hardly talked about Dad at all, but what was there to talk about? Like Mom said when we left Newbury, he was dead. We weren't. He hadn't changed a bit.

We had.

CHAPTER 15

THERE IS A WRONG WAY to do things. Dad taught me that.

I saw Roxanne picking the lock on the door to the Triple-J art room, and it was like I could hear Dad shouting it at me from beyond the grave.

"Hey!" I yelled at Roxanne. "You're going to ruin that lock."

She was twisting and jiggling an unbent paper clip inside the doorknob. She didn't even look up. "Don't worry," she said back. "I've done this a million times."

"It's not that." I dug inside my pocket. "I have the key."

"You do?"

"I have a master key for all the classroom doors."

"Where did you get that?"

"I found it in my dad's stuff."

Roxanne pushed her hair out of her face. "I

thought he'd have to turn in all his keys."

"Yeah," I said. "That's what the employee handbook says too. If you die, you have to turn your keys in. It's definitely a rule. I guess he forgot."

Roxanne shook her head. "He's going to be in big trouble."

I slipped the key into the door and unlocked it with a satisfying click. "We'll report him," I said. I pushed the door open. "After you."

Roxanne entered the room and I followed. The rich smells of oil paint and clay greeted us. Roxanne snapped a panel of switches into the on position, and rows of fluorescent bulbs hummed to life. The change from shade and shadow to bare illumination took me by surprise.

"Ouch," I said, covering my eyes.

"It's really a rotten light for an art room," said Roxanne. "Help me open the blinds."

One by one we lifted the shades and let sunlight fill the space around us. It gave texture and color and depth to the room. It made the skin on my arms and cheeks feel good when I stood in the warm glow coming through the window.

"Why the breaking and entering?" I asked.

Roxanne leaned against the window ledge. "I

wanted to show you something."

I had avoided the art rooms since my return to the Triple J. My father spent a lot of his free time painting down here. The bathroom where he died was just around the corner too. In addition, the art classrooms did not require much custodial attention during the summer. The art teachers, even though they all seemed a little flaky to me, cleaned and organized the rooms themselves before the school year began.

Roxanne pointed to the back of the room. "Look, Dulcie."

I turned to the wall where Roxanne was pointing. It was covered with art work, paintings mostly. They all seemed to have something in common, but I couldn't figure out what it was at first. I took a step closer. Step again. And suddenly, I knew.

"Your dad," Roxanne said. "It's all about your dad."

The wall was covered with framed canvases, a few drawings, and lots of matted work. There were watercolors and pastels, a couple bold oils, all obviously created by students. Some of the work was better than others. A few were really terrible, but a few more were very good.

"What is this?" I asked. "Why did people do this?"

"The art teachers loved your dad," explained

Roxanne. "Plus, it was an assignment. We were supposed to create something that showed a little of your dad's life, something that didn't have anything to do with death. I'm sure it was one of the counselor's great ideas to help us deal."

"You paint?"

"A little."

"They turned Dad's accident into homework?"

Roxanne paused. "I think that your dad would see it as a teaching opportunity that was not wasted."

"Did you come up with that yourself?"

"No," she admitted. "That's what Mr. Bricker told us. But it sounds good, and I agree with him."

Both of us were quiet for a moment.

"You know," Roxanne said, "most of us weren't traumatized or anything. We were just sad."

I nodded.

"A lot of kids still wanted to concentrate on death," Roxanne continued, "but our teacher, Mr. Densinger, said that asking high school students to think about death is like asking fish to pee in water."

"Mr. Densinger said that?"

"Yeah."

I decided to rethink my opinion of the art department.

"Which one do you like best?" asked Roxanne.

I paused. "It's a little overwhelming."

"But it's good, isn't it?"

It was good. A sort of wall of fame. A eulogy for the high school janitor. There were paintings of clean, empty hallways, a collage of photographs from last year's yearbook arranged into the profile of a man. I liked that. There was a painting of a mop and another of a girl with dark hair. I hoped that wasn't supposed to be me.

"What's that one?" I asked, pointing to a strange green image.

"I hoped you'd find it," Roxanne said, laughing.

"What is it?"

"It's called 'This is Not a Courgette.'"

"It looks like a zucchini."

"*Courgette* is another word for zucchini."

"Let me guess," I said. "Is that yours?"

Roxanne grinned. "I always thought your dad had a really big heart, and I remembered how he loved jokes and words. I looked in the dictionary for words that had something to do with heart. I found *cordate, cordiform*—they both mean heart-shaped. Then there was *courage*. Next was *courgette*. It looked like it should have something to do with heart, but it means zucchini. I thought that was funny."

"If it's not a zucchini, what is it?"

"It's a painting of something near to my heart."

I stared at the painting that was not a heart and not a zucchini. I was laughing and crying at the same time. "Thank you," I said. "I never knew I could be so moved by a vegetable."

CHAPTER 16

IT WAS A FRIDAY morning. Frank got an early start, but I overslept a little. I dragged myself through my morning routine and found a note on the kitchen table.

Hey, sleepyhead. I'll meet you at school.

"Okay," I said out loud. Even when he wasn't there, it felt like Frank was in the room.

I skipped the cornflakes and headed down the hill to swing through the Donut Stop for treats to make up for being late. It was just five minutes after eight when I put the box of donuts on Frank's desk. "Did I miss anything?" I asked.

"Is there a Boston Creme in there for me?" asked Frank.

"Of course."

"Then you didn't miss anything."

"Where's Roxanne?" I asked.

As if on cue, she appeared in the doorway. "Sorry," she said. "Sorry I'm late."

"Don't make it a habit." Frank turned to me. "Right?"

"Have a donut," I said to Roxanne.

Roxanne took a jelly-filled. She poured coffee from the pot behind my dad's old chair. When she held out her cup, I noticed a big bandage wrapped around her forearm.

"What happened to you?" I asked.

She took a bite of her donut and spoke with her mouth full. "I dropped the iron."

"We're janitors," I reminded her. "What are you ironing all the time?"

She pushed her hair out of her face. She looked more disheveled than usual. "I was just helping my mother. It was an accident."

"Your mother needs you to press her Kmart smock?" I asked.

"She's at Burger King now," said Roxanne. "Management trainee."

"She's moving up," I said.

Roxanne wiped powdered sugar off her chin. "She's chasing a dream."

"She should do her own ironing," said Frank. "If she keeps letting you do it, you're going to burn your house down."

"I wish," said Roxanne.

"Be careful what you wish for," said Frank.

Roxanne didn't answer.

"Well," Frank said slowly, "speaking of mothers, we're having company tonight."

Roxanne glanced up. She looked worried all of a sudden. "My mother?"

"No," said Frank. He slid a postcard across his desk toward me. "This was at the post office this morning."

"What is it?" I asked.

"It's a postcard."

"I can see that."

"It's for you."

I lifted the card off his desktop. It showed a fat old four-prop airliner flying over San Francisco's Golden Gate Bridge. On the reverse, a little stick-figure drawing of a woman stared up at me. The words SEE YOU FRIDAY were penciled inside a comic strip bubble above the figure's head. I read it to myself and then looked up.

"Is this supposed to be Mom?"

"Yes," said Frank.

"*My* mom?"

"Yes," he said again.

"See you Friday?"

"That's what it says."

"Today is Friday."

"I called her cell phone," said Frank. "She'll be here for supper."

"For supper?"

Frank nodded. "Tonight."

"Tonight?"

I think my brain must have gone into some sort of mental gridlock. All I could do was repeat the last thing I heard.

"I can't wait to meet her. Is she anything like Dulcie?" Roxanne asked Frank.

Frank smiled a little. "Oh, yeah."

I didn't say anything.

"Can I?" Roxanne asked me. "Would you mind? I'd love to meet a normal mom."

"A normal mom?" I said. The absurdity of the statement cleared my head. "A normal mom? Is there any such thing? Would a normal mom drag her kid three thousand miles for no reason? Would a normal mom throw away a perfectly good pickup truck? Would a normal mom fly across the whole country with no notice and just drop in?"

"That all sounds like normal-mom behavior to me," said Frank.

I retrieved a dog-eared Webster's dictionary from the shelf behind Dad's old desk. I turned through the pages until I found what I was looking for. "'Normal,'" I recited. "'Characterized by average intelligence. Free from mental disorder. The name of a town in Illinois.'" I glanced at Roxanne. "That last one is the only Normal my mom ever visited."

"Dulcie," said Frank, "I think you're confusing normal with reasonable."

I went back to the dictionary. "'Reasonable. Being within the bounds of common sense. Rational. Not excessive or extreme.'"

Frank took the book from my hands. He flipped to a new page and read out loud. "'Mother. A woman who conceives, gives birth to, and/or raises a child.'" He looked up. "There's nothing in there about normal, rational, or reasonable."

"That's no excuse," I said. "And what's with the and/or?"

"Give your mother a break," said Frank, "and/or remember that she's had just as tough a year as you."

I sighed. "I know."

Roxanne stood up and grabbed a dry-mop from a rack against the wall. "Come on," she said. "Let's get started."

I followed her to the door. "I didn't realize the mother job description was so flimsy."

Roxanne handed me a mop. "There does seem to be a lot of room for improvisation."

CHAPTER 17

IT WAS LATE when we checked the last item off Frank's to-do list. Roxanne and I were rinsing mops in the utility sink. Frank reviewed invoices and notes he'd clipped into an old three-ring binder. "Where did this summer go?" he muttered.

"School is still three weeks away," I said.

Frank lowered the binder and looked at his watch.

"Are you counting the minutes till then?" I asked.

"Your mother should be here soon," he said. "I'm going to leave now and run to the grocery store." He turned to me. "You have the truck, so you and Roxanne can meet me back at the house."

Roxanne stood up. Like me, she was covered in grime. We both smelled like floor wax and vinegar. "I don't mean to be all prim and proper," I said. "But maybe Roxanne would like clean clothes."

"Stop at her house on the way." Frank turned to Roxanne. "See if your mom wants to come for supper."

"No," Roxanne said quickly. "She has to work."

"Okay," said Frank. He tossed me the big metal key ring he kept clipped to his belt. "Make sure everything's locked up before you go."

I grabbed the ring out of the air. In addition to classroom masters, Frank's ring held keys to file cabinets, supply closets, soda machines, paper towel holders, and a hundred other locked places I'd never even thought of.

"The keys to the kingdom," I said. I rattled the keys like crazy wind chimes. "Whatever I bind on earth will be bound in heaven. Whatever I loose on earth will be loosed in heaven, right?"

Frank laughed. "You've been reading the door again."

"The gospel according to Matthew," I said. "It's just above the doorknob."

"A key," said Roxanne in her best read-aloud voice. "A very large key that opens something, some useful door, somewhere up there."

I turned and stared at her.

Roxanne smiled. "I read the door too."

"'Riding the Elevator into the Sky,'" I said. "We

read that in English last year. I taped it above the doorframe myself."

"I like it," said Roxanne. She cleared her throat and recited from memory:

"As the fireman said:
Don't book a room over the fifth floor
in any hotel in New York.
They have ladders that will reach further
but no one will climb them."

She paused.

"I would climb them," I said.

Roxanne gave me an odd look. "Dulcie," she said. "I know that."

CHAPTER 18

AFTER FRANK LEFT, Roxanne and I put the remaining buckets and mops away. We made the lock-up walk together flicking light switches, rattling doors, checking on the chemistry labs to make sure they hadn't spontaneously burst into flame. At last, we locked the loading dock doors behind us and crossed the parking lot toward the red pickup truck.

"Are you excited to see your mom?" Roxanne asked.

"Yes," I admitted. "I'm a little nervous too. What about you?"

"I'd pay money to never see her again."

I was confused, but then I realized that Roxanne was talking about her own mother.

The short ride to Roxanne's house from the Triple J only took a minute. We parked at the curb. When I turned off the engine, music blared from the Soules' open windows and doors. It was so loud that the truck's steering wheel shook in my hands.

"What is that?" I asked.

"That's my mom," said Roxanne.

"I thought you said she was working."

Roxanne was silent for a moment. "Dulcie," she said, "I lied. I don't want my mother to come to dinner."

"That's okay."

"I don't think she'd come even if I asked her," Roxanne continued. "She's really not very good company."

"Really," I said. "It's okay. I understand."

Roxanne stepped out of the truck. "I know."

The two of us walked toward the house. Drums and bass and electric guitars beat through my stomach and up my backbone. "Is she having a party in there?"

Roxanne shook her head. "Music soothes the savage beast."

"Should I wait outside?"

Roxanne stopped. "I'd rather you came in. Do you mind?"

"Lead the way."

We went to the side door that Roxanne and I had repaired a few weeks earlier. The screen was already torn again, but the frame was still attached to its hinges.

"Mom?" Roxanne called.

There was no answer. I'm sure that our voices didn't carry above the music. Roxanne pulled the door open.

On the day we'd fixed the screen door, Roxanne told me that her mother was inside napping. I'd never stepped into the house. The first thing I noticed when we entered was the smell, a combination of cats and stale food. "Ugh," I said out loud.

"Sorry," Roxanne said, embarrassed.

We walked down a little hallway. Stacks of newspaper as high as my waist leaned along the walls. "What's all this?" I asked.

"My mom tried running a paper route for a couple weeks," Roxanne explained. "She quit when she disagreed with the editorials."

"Really?"

"No," said Roxanne. "Mostly she just overslept. She wanted me to take over, but I told her I'd only deliver on days that the headlines wouldn't depress the customers."

"Looks like there wasn't too much good news here for a while."

"That's why I took the job at the Triple J," said Roxanne.

We stepped past the bundles toward a dim, dirty kitchen. An ironing board lay in the middle of the kitchen floor. The iron itself sat tipped over among a few open cereal boxes on the kitchen counter. "What happened here?" I asked.

Roxanne held out her bandaged arm. "Ironing disaster."

I followed Roxanne into a living room where the music blasted. A small stereo sat on a squat coffee table beneath a picture window. There was a charcoal-colored sofa and a rocking chair in there too. A couple dozen CDs and their cases littered the floor around two speakers that sat one on either side of the coffee table. To the right of the picture window, a door led to the front yard. A metal rake and a garden spade leaned against the wall.

"Doing some gardening in here?" I asked.

"What?" shouted Roxanne above the din.

I walked over to the stereo, found the power switch, and shut it off. The sudden silence felt shocking and good. "Are you doing some gardening?" I asked again.

Roxanne pointed out the window. I could see Dad's pickup truck parked near the street. For the first time, I noticed that the front yard had been raked clean. Roxanne had trimmed back the bushes. She'd planted a row of chrysanthemums and a few hydrangeas too.

"That looks nice," I told her.

"Frank let me borrow the tools. I like plants."

"I remember," I said. "You're the Johnny Appleseed of weeding."

I was about to compliment Roxanne's landscaping skills some more, when a voice interrupted us from upstairs. "Who shut off the music? Roxanne, is that you?"

Roxanne stood in the doorway between the living room and the kitchen. For a second, she looked like she might run away. Before she could decide, Mrs. Soule thumped down the stairs into the living room. She looked angry and a little unsteady on her feet. She had a bandage over one eye. She was focused on the stereo, and she didn't turn to greet us.

I stepped forward to say hello.

Without warning, the woman reached out and hit me.

I have not been hit often in my life. My father swatted my bottom once when I was nine years old because I leaped off our roof into a huge snowbank. I

124

had big snow pants on then, and I'd landed safely. As an added bonus, the pants prevented me from feeling most of the spanking. Another time, Frank clocked me with a two-by-four when we were loading lumber in the truck. It was an accident, but it hurt a lot. The worst blow was the time my head bounced off a school bus window during a field trip. The driver had to brake hard to avoid a deer. My ears rang for a week.

But none of those experiences prepared me for the short, powerful, almost casual jab that Mrs. Soule planted on my chest. I stumbled back on my feet and tripped onto the sofa. I sank hard onto the cushions, and a cloud of dust and cat fur flew up around me. I couldn't believe what had just happened.

"Mom!" Roxanne cried.

Mrs. Soule looked surprised. "What?"

"You hit Dulcie!" Roxanne yelled.

Mrs. Soule glanced back and forth between us for a second. Quickly, I understood that she'd meant to punch Roxanne, but that didn't make me feel any better. I wanted to protest. At least holler something rude. But I discovered that I could not exhale. *"Etch,"* I managed to gasp. *"Etch!"*

"Etch?" asked Mrs. Soule.

"She can't breathe!" Roxanne hollered. She

stepped over and rubbed my back. "Don't talk, Dulcie. She knocked the wind out of you. Catch your breath."

"Sorry," Mrs. Soule mumbled. "I didn't realize it was you."

My lungs and throat burned. My eyes filled with tears.

"What did you do that for?" Roxanne yelled at her mother.

"I told you not to touch the stereo," said Mrs. Soule.

Roxanne stepped toward her mother. It appeared that the two of them were about to have a fistfight, and based on the pain in my chest, I was pretty certain that Mrs. Soule would pummel Roxanne badly. I struggled to my feet, took a step toward them, and that's when I planted my foot on one of those plastic CD cases lying around. The thing shot out from beneath me like a banana peel in a cartoon. I flew into the air like thousands of animated dimwits before me. I even had my own sound effects. First there was my screaming, next a ripping sound as my foot blasted through one of the stereo speakers, and then a sort of thud when my backside hit the floor.

"What the hell!" shouted Mrs. Soule. She

glanced at the speaker and then turned toward me in an obvious rage. Quickly, Roxanne stepped around her mother, grabbed the garden shovel off the wall, and swung it through the front of the second speaker. It died with a muffled *woof*.

"What are you doing!" screamed Mrs. Soule.

Roxanne lifted the shovel and stepped toward the AM/FM/CD player on the coffee table. It never had a chance. She pounded on the plastic box. Tiny knobs and dials flew around the room. "Wait! Wait!" I tried to shout, but I couldn't make sounds.

Roxanne stopped when she noticed me waving. "What?"

I pointed at the electric cord that still connected the stereo to a wall socket. "Electrocute," I croaked.

Roxanne nodded. "Thanks." She pulled the plug from the wall, turned back to the stereo, and then hammered it into rubble.

"Stop it!" Mrs. Soule yelled, but Roxanne had found a sort of rhythm of destruction. *Lift, swing, smash. Lift, swing, smash.* She worked like a railroad hand driving spikes into the earth or a lumberjack chopping down a giant sequoia. She'd reached the coffee table now and was using the edge of the spade to hack it in two.

Mrs. Soule stood locked in place. I watched Roxanne in awe. This was much more impressive than stealing a truck while the whole world slept. "Stop it!" her mother shouted again.

"No!"

Mrs. Soule's hand shot out, and she socked her daughter hard.

Roxanne paused to face her mother. Roxanne's hair was not pulled back anymore. The sun coming through the picture window created an angry red halo around her face. She had the shovel raised, and for a second, I thought she was going to bring it down on her mother's head. I imagined the clank of it when it struck Mrs. Soule's skull, the way the woman's knees would buckle, and how everybody would understand that Roxanne had done exactly right thing.

"Roxanne," wailed Mrs. Soule, suddenly afraid. "I am your mother!"

Roxanne stopped. She'd choked up on the handle of the shovel, and she stood there holding it like a baseball bat. Mrs. Soule said nothing. She opened her mouth. Her teeth were brown from coffee and cigarettes. For a moment it looked as if she might speak, but then she stopped.

She turned away.

She retreated up the stairs and left us standing in a filthy room with a couple borrowed garden tools and a broken radio.

Roxanne gave the coffee table a kick. It split in half and collapsed onto the floor. "Like I said before," Roxanne explained. "My mother is not very good dinner company."

"I'm sorry," I said. "I'm so sorry."

"It's okay," said Roxanne.

"You should have left me outside." I was babbling. "I'll pay for the speakers."

"You have no money."

"I made things worse."

Roxanne shook her head. "It would have been worse if you weren't here. You should see her when she gets really mad."

I took a breath. "No thanks."

Roxanne dug a toe into one of the broken speakers. It tipped over onto its side. "When I was little, my mother used to teach me the words to songs. I went to school, and the other kids knew 'Three Blind Mice' and 'The Farmer in the Dell.' I walked around the playground waving my arms and screaming, 'I am iron man.'"

I looked at her blankly.

"Heavy metal songs," Roxanne explained. "My mother thought it was funny. I was always in trouble for singing them at school, but as long as it made my mother laugh, I wouldn't stop. I loved to make my mother laugh."

"She's got a wicked sense of humor."

"I don't think anybody ever explained the whole parenting thing to her. Actually, I don't think anybody ever explained the whole being a grown-up thing to her."

I didn't speak.

"She got fired from Kmart," Roxanne said. "She didn't quit. She got mad at some woman whose kid was screaming in the customer service line. Mom stuck a CD into the stereo display and blasted it."

Roxanne moved junk around on the floor with the shovel. She picked up a broken CD case and handed it to me. Another oldie but goodie. "The Ramones," I read. "My Dad liked the Ramones."

"They were really very good, but if you play their song 'Beat on the Brat' while you're working at the Kmart customer service desk, the management team there will not be happy."

"I see," I said, but I didn't really.

"Mom stole the stereo when they fired her," said

Roxanne. "Nobody stopped her, but I think she grabbed a defective one."

"Why do you think that?" I asked.

She pointed to the rubble at our feet. "It doesn't work anymore."

CHAPTER 19

ROXANNE AND I left the mess at her house and headed to Frank's. We didn't speak much.

Lightning bugs flickered around the dim houses that we passed. The smell of barbecue and the distant pop of leftover fireworks drifted toward us from a hundred backyards. Summer really was coming to an end.

It was nearly dark when I pulled the red Chevy into Frank's driveway. A figure stood up from the shadows on the front porch. It was my grandfather.

"We're really late," said Roxanne. "I hope he's not mad."

"He might be," I said. Frank hated being late. "But he'll get over it."

We stepped down from the cab. Frank didn't speak.

"Hi," I said.

He nodded. "Your mother's inside."

"I'm sorry we took so long."

"We already ate," he said. "She's near tears in there. She thinks you don't want to see her."

"I do want to see her," I said. "We had a problem."

"A problem?" he asked.

"It was my fault," Roxanne interrupted.

Just then, Mom came to the screen door behind Frank. "Dulcie?"

"Mom?" My heart started to beat in my chest like a revved-up engine. Mom stepped out onto the porch, and I walked up the steps. Before I could say a word, my mother reached out and wrapped me in a hug. "Hi," I said into Mom's shoulder.

"Hey," Mom said.

I still smelled like the Triple J. Mom felt wrinkled and soft. Her hair was back to its original pretty blond, but it sagged a little on her shoulders. She seemed tired, and for a moment, neither of us spoke. Finally, I took a step back. "Hi," I said again.

Mom grinned. "We already did that part."

"Mom," I said, "this is my friend Roxanne."

Mom turned to Roxanne. I wondered if she noticed the lines that tears had traced down Roxanne's dirty cheeks. "It's nice to finally meet you," Mom said.

"You're really pretty," said Roxanne. Neither Mom nor I expected that. Roxanne brushed hair out of her eyes. "Dulcie didn't tell me you were pretty."

"Where did you find this girl?" Mom asked.

"In the weeds," I said.

"In the flowers," said Roxanne.

Mom laughed. "I like her."

"Me too," I said. "I'm really sorry we took so long."

"That's okay," said Mom.

"What was the problem?" Frank asked.

I glanced quickly at Roxanne.

"You said you had a problem," said Frank. "Do I need to run over to the school and fix something?"

I shook my head. "No."

Roxanne looked doubtful. She stared down at her dirty shoes. She was still dressed in sweaty work clothes and paint-stained sneakers. Her shirt had a big black mark on one sleeve, and her jeans were nearly worn through to her knees. I stepped toward her and put a hand on her shoulder. "I think you should tell."

"What is it?" said Frank.

Roxanne took a big breath and then let it out. "It's my mother."

"Problems with your mother," said Frank. "Dulcie

is sort of an expert in that department."

"Dulcie tried to help me," said Roxanne.

"It didn't go very well," I said.

"What happened?" asked Mom.

Neither Roxanne nor I spoke. Finally, Roxanne held up her arm. "This morning," she said. "My mother tried to iron the wrinkles out of my arm."

CHAPTER 20

WE SAT AT FRANK'S kitchen table while Roxanne told the whole story. Big quiet tears rolled down her face. She described a house filled with yelling and filth and violence. "I can't wait to come to work in the morning," she said.

"Then it must be really bad," Frank teased her gently.

Roxanne rubbed a sleeve across her nose and smudged dirt across her cheeks. "I like being a janitor. It's the only time I can clean things up."

Mom stood. She found a paper towel, ran it under the faucet for a moment, and began to dab Roxanne's face. It was such a gentle thing to do. It made Roxanne cry even harder. "It's just gotten worse lately."

"What happened with the iron?" asked Mom.

"My mother threw it at me," said Roxanne. "She doesn't have very good aim. Plus she forgot to unplug it. When it reached the end of the cord, it flew back and bounced off her face. It made her so angry. She grabbed me before I could run out of the room."

"The day you had your fingers all bandaged up," I said. "What happened then?"

"She threw the iron that day too." Roxanne wiggled her fingers. "I caught it. I won't make that mistake again."

"How long has this been going on?" asked Mom.

"A long time." Roxanne looked at the floor and then at Frank. "I wanted to tell you." She turned to me. "I told your dad. He was so nice. He said he was going to help me." She paused. "But then he died."

I felt my face get red. I noticed Mom turn the same color as me.

"I wish he hadn't done that," Roxanne said.

"Me too," Mom said. I reached over and put my hand on Mom's back. I felt her lean on me just a little.

"I think things will be better soon," said Roxanne

"Really?" said Mom.

Roxanne shrugged.

"Roxanne," Frank said gently. "What if they're not?"

Roxanne wasn't crying anymore, but it looked like she wanted to. I know I did. "I don't know," said Roxanne. "Sometimes I get scared. I don't think she'd ever really hurt me."

Mom put a hand on Roxanne and her shoulders sagged. "Honey," said Mom. "She's already really hurting you."

After that, Frank told us to wash up. Roxanne and I did our best to scrub off the dirt and grime and ugly feelings we'd collected at her house. We walked into the kitchen, and Frank placed a huge bowl of spaghetti in the middle of the table. "Sit," he said.

I'd found clean clothes. Roxanne was taller than me and took the Cal Bears sweats that mom offered. "I'm not really hungry," Roxanne said to Frank. "Would you mind if I just lie down?"

Frank led Roxanne to the living room couch. She closed her eyes and fell asleep almost immediately.

I sat at the kitchen table. The room was filled with the smells of fresh tomato sauce and grated cheese. I took a bite of pasta. Mom sat across the table. Quietly, she pushed a small package toward me.

"What's this?" I asked.

"A present," she said softly.

"For me?"

Mom nodded. "New underwear. I remember you lost a bunch."

I laughed out loud. Probably too loud and too hard, but it felt good just the same.

"How's the Volvo?" I asked.

"Good," said Mom. "I put an earthquake bag in the trunk."

"Is that like an airbag?"

"It's just a backpack," she explained. "You fill it with emergency supplies. Things like water, some food, a couple rolls of toilet paper."

"You'll need more than a couple rolls when California falls into the ocean," said Frank.

"Have you felt any earthquakes?" I asked.

"Just a tremor. It was nothing." Mom whispered so she wouldn't wake Roxanne. "But I almost peed my pants."

Frank shook his head. "You really want to stay there?"

"I've made some friends. I like it a lot." Mom looked at me. "I'd like it more if I didn't live alone."

"You want to yell at me?" I asked.

"You think I should?" asked Mom.

"Probably," I admitted.

"You're probably right."

"Let me help," I said. "What was I thinking? Stealing the truck, running away from home, driving around America all by myself."

"That's a good start," Mom said.

"I could have gotten myself killed or lost or worse. I could have run out of gas in Pittsburgh. If you could, you'd put me over your knee and give me a good spanking."

Mom looked surprised. "I never spanked you."

"I never stole a truck."

"You couldn't reach the pedals," said Frank

Mom shrugged. "Things change."

"Even if I could have reached the pedals, I wouldn't have gone anywhere," I said. "Why would I? I was surrounded by people I love." I looked at Frank. "People that love me. What changed about that?"

Mom sighed.

"Do I have to go back to California?" I asked.

Mom took a slow breath. "Dulcie," she said. "I didn't come here to kidnap you again."

"I don't have to go back?"

Mom shook her head. "No."

Even Frank was quiet then. Suddenly, I wasn't sure if I had just won something or lost something.

"Mrs. Jones?" It was Roxanne. We hadn't even noticed that she was awake.

"Yes," said Mom.

"I was wondering. Could you kidnap me?"

CHAPTER 21

THE BROKEN SCREEN on Roxanne's door looked like an ugly gray tongue sticking out at me. It dared me to rap my knuckles on the frame. I could not get my hand to do it.

"Go on," Mom said to me. "Knock on the door."

I didn't move. I wished Frank was with us.

Mom reached over my shoulder and banged on the screen door. "Hello!" she called.

"What if they're not awake?" I asked.

We heard a crash somewhere inside the house.

"They're awake," said Mom.

Roxanne appeared in the doorway disheveled and out of breath. She'd slept on Frank's couch until just before the sun came up, then snuck back home knowing we'd be visiting soon. "My mother never sees the sun rise," Roxanne had promised. "She usually gets up around the crack of eleven."

"Hi," I said when Roxanne appeared in the doorway.

"Hi."

"Good morning, Roxanne," said Mom. "Would you tell your mother we're here?"

Roxanne nodded and quickly disappeared down the hallway. Mom opened the door and let herself in. I followed. The view hadn't changed and if anything, the smell was even worse. Mom just shook her head. In the kitchen, she pulled two chairs away from the table, swept crumbs from the seats, and ordered me to sit. "I'm sure Mrs. Soule will be right in."

The floor creaked above us, and then Mrs. Soule's cranky voice spoke to Roxanne at the end of the hall. "Who? Who wants to see me? What do they want?"

I watched Mom put a smile on her face. It was as if she had reached into a bag and pulled out a mask. Even if you didn't know her, you could tell that the expression was not a real one. Her body was rigid and stiff. Her shoulders and back were knotted up like she was about to chop down a dead tree. You'd have to be blind to think this was a happy lady. I pushed my chair as far back away from her as possible.

Mrs. Soule appeared by herself in the kitchen doorway. She was wearing the same gray sweats and sweatshirt I'd seen on her the night before. "Hello?"

"Francine Soule," Mom said. "It's been a while,

hasn't it?" Mom stood up like she was going to go and hug the madwoman in front of us. "It's Annie Morrigan Jones."

"I know who you are," said Mrs. Soule.

"How have you been?" asked Mom.

"A lot like you."

"Really?"

"I'm raising a daughter all by myself," said Mrs. Soule.

"That's what I hear," said Mom.

"My husband wasn't as thoughtful as yours, though."

"Why do you say that?"

"Mine didn't die."

Mom shrugged. "Men," she said.

Mrs. Soule studied Mom and me for a moment. "Why are you in my house?"

"I moved to California," Mom said. "I came back for a couple days to visit my father. Dulcie is staying with him now. I understand that she and Roxanne have become friends." Mom looked slowly around the room. "I came to say thank you for keeping an eye on her."

Mrs. Soule glared at me. I'm sure she was trying to decide whether or not I'd told anyone about what had happened between us. "She seems like a good kid."

That took me by surprise.

"Roxanne too," said Mom.

"Really?" said Mrs. Soule. She crossed the kitchen and leaned against the greasy stove. "How would you know that?"

Mom found her chair and sat down again. "My dad speaks highly of her. My husband did too."

"Well, there's a couple of experts."

I bit my lip.

"I'm sure you've been very kind to Dulcie," Mom said.

Yeah, right, I thought.

"I wonder if I might return the favor," Mom continued.

"What do you mean?"

"I'd like to take Roxanne with me to California," Mom said.

"Are you kidding?"

"No."

Mrs. Soule laughed like a dog barking. "Roxanne isn't going anywhere. Summer's almost over. School starts in a few weeks. I don't have money to send her on some California vacation."

"I'm not talking about a vacation," Mom said.

"What are you talking about?" Mrs. Soule asked warily.

"I can't get my daughter to leave Newbury," Mom said. "According to Dulcie, Newbury is heaven on earth."

"It's a real paradise," said Mrs. Soule.

"Not for everybody." We hadn't noticed Roxanne arrive in the doorway. She had a hand on the door frame for support.

"What's that supposed to mean?" asked Mrs. Soule.

"It means I want to move to California," said Roxanne.

"What?" said Mrs. Soule.

"Please, Mom." Roxanne spoke quickly. "This is a good idea. This will be good for both of us."

"With Dulcie staying here," said Mom, "I have plenty of room. Roxanne could stay with me."

"You mean live with you?" asked Mrs. Soule.

"That's right."

Mrs. Soule said nothing. She looked angry and confused. Then she shook her head and turned toward Roxanne. "Are you out of your mind?"

"No, Mom."

"Whose idea was this?" Mrs. Soule turned to Mom, then to me. "Did you put this in her head?"

"Francine—" said Mom.

"Roxanne isn't going anywhere," said Mrs. Soule. She turned to Roxanne and hollered, "Do you hear me? You're not going anywhere. You are staying right here."

"She doesn't need your permission," I said, trying unsuccessfully to keep my voice from trembling.

"Then why did you ask?"

Mom stood up from the kitchen table. "We were trying to be polite, Francine."

"Roxanne is my daughter," said Mrs. Soule. "She'll do what I say."

Mom stepped forward. "What if she doesn't, Francine? What are you going to do about it?"

"She's my daughter." Mrs. Soule's voice rose even higher.

"You hurt her," I shouted.

Mom put her hand on my shoulder. "Dulcie," she warned.

"Who says I hurt my daughter?" Mrs. Soule turned to where Roxanne had been standing, but Roxanne had fled the room.

"Dulcie just said so," said Mom. "I believe her."

"What do you know?"

"My husband knew. My father knows too."

"I haven't seen your husband lately," said Mrs. Soule. "And your father is an old nut who hangs around a high school all day talking to teenage girls. Is that even legal?"

Mom turned to me. "Let's go, Dulcie."

I wanted to say one more thing to Roxanne's mother, something mean and ugly, but before I could, the sound of an engine roaring to life came from outside the house. Mom didn't even look at Mrs. Soule. She turned and walked toward the front room that Roxanne and I had destroyed the day before. I followed her and heard a loud backfire from an exhaust pipe near the road. It was the sound an old V-8 would make if somebody crushed the gas pedal to the floor.

Mom opened the front door and pointed. "Francine," she said, "your daughter is stealing our truck."

"What?" Mrs. Soule went to the front window. She had to step over the dead radio to get there. Through the window, we could see the big red pickup, its transmission clunking through the gears, fishtail away from us. A cloud of dust billowed up behind it.

"What's going on?" Mrs. Soule hollered.

"Roxanne!" I shouted at the window. I knew she couldn't hear me, but I couldn't help myself. "Be careful!"

"You've scared that child into doing something stupid," Mom said quietly.

Mrs. Soule turned to me. "You had something to do with this."

I shook my head. "No."

Mom dug through her purse until a cell phone tumbled out of the bag. I picked it up. "Dulcie," Mom said, "call your grandfather."

"If you really think my daughter is stealing that truck, you should call the cops," said Mrs. Soule. "That will teach her."

I stood still, unsure of who to call.

"Dulcie," Mom said sharply, "dial the phone."

"Roxanne better not be running away," Mrs. Soule added. Her eyes were a pale, fading blue, empty of everything but rage. "She better not."

I punched in Frank's number and listened to the phone ring. I closed my eyes and thought about Roxanne. Somehow I just knew that she was not running away in my father's truck. She knew what the truck meant to me. Not only that, she was more than clever enough to invent her own thrilling getaway plan if that's what she wanted to do. Mom had to be right. Roxanne was just plain scared.

"Hello," Frank sang into the phone.

"Frank," I said, "it's me."

"How's it going?" he asked.

"Not good."

"You need me to come over?"

I glanced at the two women, big, angry she-wolves, pacing around the room. "Yeah."

"Anything I should know?"

I took a breath. "Mrs. Soule said no. Roxanne stole Dad's truck, and somebody looks like she's going to commit murder any minute now."

"Which somebody?"

"I'm not sure."

"I'm on my way."

I hung up on Frank and lowered the phone.

"Dulcie," said Mom, "where do you think Roxanne will go?"

"Where is she?" asked Mrs. Soule.

I shook my head. Both Frank's house and the Triple J were too obvious. She could just be driving around. That's probably what I would have done. And then it came to me. "Sometimes Roxanne and I visit Dad at the cemetery."

"So?" asked Mrs. Soule.

"We like it there."

"The cemetery?" said Mrs. Soule. "With dead people?"

Mom finally lost her cool. "Dead people don't burn their children with steam irons!" she hollered. Mom snatched the phone out of my hand. "I think I will call the police."

For the first time, Mrs. Soule looked something other than angry. She was afraid, and she had good reason to be.

Mom muttered to herself while she held the phone to her ear. "For the love of God," she said, "who put the monkeys in charge of the zoo?"

CHAPTER 22

WE WAITED AWKWARDLY in the front yard for
Frank to arrive in his station wagon. When he pulled
up, Mom, Mrs. Soule, and I piled into the car. The
backseat was folded down and filled with work stuff,
so Mom had to sit in my lap. I wrapped my arms
around her waist and buried my head in her hair
while Frank drove.

We arrived at the cemetery and circled past Dad
and Gram and all our dead neighbors. "This is stupid,"
said Mrs. Soule, but she didn't sound so sure of herself any longer.

"There," said Frank.

Two lines of tire tracks led off the cemetery road
and across a wet field that had not yet been turned
into gravesites. The tire marks crossed the grass and
continued directly over the top of a small embank-
ment at the opposite end of the small green. Frank
pulled his station wagon into the grass and bounced

across the field. He stopped the car at the top of the incline.

On the other side of that bank, there was a small, black pond. A hopper, Frank called it. Newbury was dotted with various bodies of water just like it. There was a wooden bench beside the cemetery hopper. Roxanne and I drove up here in the truck and ate our lunch beside the pond sometimes.

Frank, Mom, Mrs. Soule, and I tumbled out of the wagon and stood atop the slight hill. From the crest, we could see the water just a few steps below. The truck's tire marks went straight into the pond. A thin film of gasoline and oil floated on the water's surface.

"Oh, my God," said Mom.

"What happened?" Mrs. Soule screamed.

I ran to the water's edge. Frank ran back to the rear of his station wagon. He opened the gate and pulled out a long rope. Mom and Mrs. Soule stepped toward the hopper. I turned to see what Frank was doing. That's when I saw the soaking wet red-haired girl sitting on the opposite shore.

"Hey," I shouted without thinking.

Mom saw her, but Mrs. Soule was too busy screaming at the water to notice. Frank jogged back to me. He'd traded the rope for a ratty old sheet that we used as a paint tarp sometimes. He shoved the sheet into my arms. "Quick. Go wrap her up."

I took the sheet and walked toward Roxanne. I approached her with the same calm steps I'd seen the Kansas farm lady use when she didn't want to frighten her fainting goats. For some reason, the thought of stupid Dorothy and the wizard of Oz came into my head. This is what it felt like to pull back the curtain and find the wizard, I thought. But instead of finding a Kansas con man pulling the levers, we found something much more upsetting. When we pulled back the curtain, there was no wizard. There was nobody. There was just us.

"Hey," I said to Roxanne, more quietly this time.

Roxanne didn't answer.

I sat down in the dirt beside her. "You okay?"

She shrugged. "I killed your truck," she said.

I nodded. "That's okay."

"I'm so sorry."

I folded the sheet around Roxanne's shoulders like angel's wings. Quietly, she and I stared at the hopper for what seemed like a long time. Despite the summer heat, it struck me that we were all skating on very thin ice. We could fall into the water at any moment. On one side of the ice, we were sane and caring and careful. On the other side, we tortured children, we drove trucks into cemetery ponds, we lost people we loved when they stopped to clean scuff marks off of lavatory floors. Big fat tears rolled down Roxanne's cheeks and mixed with the pond water on her face. "It was an accident," she said.

"It's okay," I said again.

"It was your father's," she said. "I shouldn't have—"

"It was just a truck. I'll get over it." I put an arm around Roxanne.

From our seat on the ground, Roxanne and I could see that Frank and Mom had guided Mrs. Soule back to the station wagon. The police officer that Mom called had arrived.

"I better go talk to her," said Roxanne.

"Now?"

Roxanne nodded, so I took her hand and helped her to her feet. The water in the hopper was still restless and bubbly from swallowing the truck. Frank was explaining the situation to the officer when Mrs. Soule saw Roxanne and me approaching. Suddenly, her sobs were replaced by an explosive string of curse words. The police officer who had been preparing to console a grieving mother was suddenly involved in an attempt to control an insane person.

Roxanne continued to walk toward her mother. As we got closer, the swearing got worse. "Mrs. Soule," the police officer hollered unpleasantly. "I will restrain you if you don't calm down."

"I'd like to see you try it," she said.

The officer removed a pair of handcuffs from his belt.

Mrs. Soule jerked her hands over her head. "I'm calm. I'm calm already." She turned to Roxanne. "When you get home—"

"No," said Roxanne.

"You listen to me," Mrs. Soule spat out.

Roxanne shook her head. She turned to the police officer and held out her arm. Her bandage wasn't there anymore. A terrible weepy burn stood out among a few other scabs and scars. Roxanne pointed at her mother. "She did this to me."

The officer leaned forward and examined Roxanne's arm. "That's a second-degree burn."

"Shaped just like an iron," said Frank.

The police officer turned to Mrs. Soule.

"I didn't do that," she snarled.

"I didn't ask," he said. The officer, already no fan

of Roxanne's mother, snapped handcuffs onto Mrs. Soule's fleshy wrists, popped her into the open police cruiser, and slammed the door. "We'll work this out at the station."

"We'll meet you there," said Frank.

As the police cruiser pulled out of the cemetery, Roxanne spoke to my mom. "I'm sorry about the truck. I just had to get away."

Mom glanced at me before she answered Roxanne. "I understand that."

CHAPTER 23

IF THIS WERE A MOVIE, I'd end with a scene of me putting Roxanne Soule on a train to California. There'd be a star-freckled night sky, and steam hanging around a silver passenger liner at the station. Two long blasts, more like a foghorn than a train whistle, and a conductor in a smart black uniform would announce departure time. Roxanne would board the train. We'd exchange final farewells through the half-open window above her seat. The locomotive would pull away from the platform, but I wouldn't run after it. Roxanne is my friend, but chasing a train for one last good-bye is a stupid thing to do. Even in a movie, I'm sure that I would trip or run into a lamppost or something.

But this was not a movie.

Before summer was over, Roxanne turned eighteen. For her birthday, my mother and Frank bought her an airplane ticket to California. I still had no money, so

I baked a cake. Mrs. Soule did not come to the party.

By then, we'd invited Roxanne to move into Frank's house. Not long after that, she moved to California with my mom.

"I hope you don't mind that I sort of adopted your family," Roxanne told me.

"I don't mind," I promised.

Once she left, I spent a lot of time washing windows, buffing floors, and pulling weeds. Inside the Triple J, the squeal and echo of my shoes on linoleum, the hushy sounds of my breathing, the *zoosh-zoosh* of blue jeans when I walked, they all roared in my ears and made the hallways feel haunted and huge.

I passed the bathroom where Dad had his accident. I was tempted to go in and have a little quiet time, but then I figured that visiting the cemetery was weird enough. I'd begun to enjoy the visits to the big pink stone. What if I started enjoying an occasional stopover in the art department lavatory too? That would be too much.

In between talking to Frank and doing my job, I spent a lot of time staring into the big oak and glass trophy case in the main lobby of the Triple J. Frank found me there a couple weeks after Roxanne moved to California. The case was the first thing visitors saw when they came through the front doors of the school. The back panel was a mirror, so that when you looked inside it, you could see your own face alongside the blue ribbons and silver cups and framed awards.

Dad's favorite item in the case had always been the key to Newbury. It was a large gold skeleton key that sat on a small pedestal in front of a yellowed newspaper clipping. A brass plaque on the pedestal held an inscription. "This key is presented to our city's heroes that they may always call Newbury, Connecticut, their home."

Frank joined me as I studied that key. Behind it, a framed newspaper told the story of Jamie Snyder, a sophomore student at John Jacob Jerome High School in March of 1978. On her way home from school, she walked past Newbury's Birge Street skating pond. The pond, actually another hopper like the one at the cemetery, had begun to melt in the early spring sun.

On that day, Jamie Snyder heard a boy, young Brian Fox, crying for help. Brian, known to friends and family as Laserboy because of his intense devotion to anything related to *Star Wars*, had fallen through the ice after chasing a space toy he'd slid across the surface of the pond.

Jamie did not run out onto the ice to save Laserboy. Instead, she stepped out into the middle of Birge Street and forced traffic to stop. She pulled drivers out of their cars and urged them to create a human chain out onto the ice. Under the girl's direction, ten complete strangers worked together to save the child.

"Do you know why Jamie Snyder was a hero?" Frank asked me.

I studied the display a moment longer. "Because she saved that kid's life?"

Frank wiped a spot off the glass with his sleeve. "Because she turned everybody around her into heroes too."

I nodded. "When they grew up, I think Jamie Snyder and Laserboy fell in love, got married, and lived happily ever after."

"They did," said Frank.

"Really?"

"I don't know," Frank admitted. "But it was nice of her to let us keep the key in the trophy case."

"Does it really open anything?"

"It's the key to the city," said Frank. "It opens everything."

I knew Frank was teasing, but I couldn't help staring at the thing and wondering. In my pocket, I could feel Dad's old master key digging into my thigh. The keys made me think about all the doors and locks and secret places in my little town.

"I wouldn't want a key to everything," I said.

Frank nodded. "I bet Jamie Snyder felt the same way. That's why she had us lock it up."

I glanced at Frank. "But whoever has the key to the trophy case—"

Frank finished my thought. "—could unlock the whole world."

"Who has the key to the trophy case?" I asked.

Frank gave me a grin. "I haven't seen that thing in years."

He walked away, but I could hear the keys on his belt jingle-jangle for a long time.

Later, I sat at Dad's old desk and dialed the number to Mom's apartment. I thought I might leave a quick message on the answering machine, but Roxanne surprised me by picking up the call.

"Don't you guys go out?" I asked.

"I just walked in," she said. "Your mom took me shopping for school clothes, and then she went to work."

I felt a mild stab of envy, but I pushed it away. Even if the cost had been a little higher than I'd expected, I was still exactly where I wanted to be.

"Is my mom driving you crazy?" I asked.

"She mostly drives herself crazy worrying about you," said Roxanne. "She helped me sign up for school on Friday."

"You okay?"

"A little nervous," said Roxanne, "but I met the school's head janitor. His name is Mr. Alabama Vest. He told me that his great-great-great-grandfather invented the kazoo."

"You're kidding."

"Nope."

"Do you believe him?"

"Who cares?" said Roxanne. "I start weeding out the flower beds tomorrow."

We said good-bye, and I left the Triple J through the rear loading dock. Frank had left a couple hours earlier. I let him know that I felt like reading awhile and then I'd walk home. I pulled the doors shut, made sure they latched, and started to walk.

When I felt headlights on my back or saw a car coming in the distance, I stepped into the shadows or turned up a side street. I cut between two yards and hiked up a grassy bank toward a set of tall evergreens. In a couple minutes, I was standing atop a big knoll, a sort of stone outcrop at the center of Newbury's Dunstan Park, named after some guy that nobody remembered anymore.

Frank used to take me on short hikes inside Dunstan Park when I was a kid. I remembered him standing on top of the knoll. "This is the highest spot in Newbury," he said. "Smack in the middle of town."

I lay down on my back for a moment and stared up at the evening stars. As sunlight faded, more constellations would come into view. Cassiopeia, Sagittarius, Pegasus near the horizon. I felt like Snoopy on top of his doghouse. Even better, I was Snoopy on top of the world.

I tilted my head and imagined my nose about even with the Triple J. I stretched out my left hand and pointed toward Mom and Roxanne in California. My right hand held an invisible line that went straight to Frank's house. If my feet were connected to wires, long rays could stretch from me all the way to Sister Clare or to the Kansas Fainting Goat Farm. Somewhere, there was a line to the pink cemetery stones too. All these things were connected to me, and for one brief moment I was at the center of things—my town, my story, my self.

I got back to my feet and looked down again at Newbury. One of the lights below was Frank's kitchen. He was almost certainly waiting for me. He'd probably cooked something delicious, and when I walked into the house, it would smell wonderful, still hot on the pink kitchen tile.

I thought again about all the lines, real and imaginary, that surrounded me. I was not sure whether they were strands in a giant web or huge broad strokes in a picture so close to my face that I could not see it clearly.

I pointed myself downhill. From up here, I could see the dark square of Newbury's town green, the silhouettes of steeples, the simple grid of a dozen neighborhood blocks, even the soft glow from parking lot lights outside the Triple J.

I walked through the park and then through the dim streets of town. I let my feet carry me back toward Frank's house, where a waterlogged pickup sat drip-drying in Frank's garage.

Roxanne hadn't killed it after all.

Frank had a friend with a tow truck, and together we'd pulled the Chevy out of the hopper. Frank let me know that it wouldn't run for a while. "But don't worry," he promised. "We'll fix it over the winter."

"You think we'll have it running by next summer?" I asked.

"Are you planning on going somewhere?" asked Frank.

"Not today," I said. "But by then, who knows?"

ACKNOWLEDGMENTS

If you want to know the truth, I should send tuition checks to writers like Joan Bauer, Kate DiCamillo, Christopher Paul Curtis, Bruce Brooks, Patricia Reilly Giff, Roddy Doyle, Laurie Halse Anderson, and many, many others for all the lessons I've gleaned from their work. They have shown me stories and treasures that I could never discover on my own. The same should be said of my parents, my grandparents, and my sister, Michelle. I owe a special debt to children's librarians in Bristol, Connecticut; Bethlehem, Pennsylvania; Hayward, California,; Hellertown, Pennsylvania; Christiana, Pennsylvania; and Quakertown, Pennsylvania. My good friends and fellow library-lovers Brian and Jamie Fox lent me their names (and so much more!). World-famous triathlete Ginger Bethe gave me great advice and fainting goats too. Friends and coworkers at Moravian College have given me incredible encouragement and support (Go, Hounds!). Greg Lasalle, John McLaughlin, and Geriann McLaughlin give me hope, insight, and direction every day, as does my great friend, guru, and best man, Scott Hardek. I would have never been able to write this book without the constant laughter, adventure, love, and encouragement I receive from my wife, Debbie, and my children, Nicholas and Gabrielle, who make me happy every single day. After all these years, I finally get to acknowledge the greatest typing teacher in the world, Mrs. Sharon Mielcarz, of St. Paul Catholic High School in Bristol, Connecticut. Also, my heartfelt thanks to the remarkable people who make up the Rutgers University Council on Children's Literature, the Society of Children's Book Writers & Illustrators, and all the great folks at Dial Books whose work continues to bring Dulcie to life. Finally, I want to acknowledge in a very special way my editor, Nancy Mercado, whose faith, friendship, and passion for great books has inspired me from the moment we first met. You are the best. *Thank you.*